Return to

Sleepy Hollow

Dax Varley

Return to Sleepy Hollow

Copyright 2014 by Dax Varley

This book is a work of fiction. All characters, incidents, and dialogue are drawn from the author's imagination and are not to be construed as real. Any resemblance to actual events or persons, living or dead, is entirely coincidental

Part One

Philadelphia

February 1794

He was there again…just below. I awoke as always to the power of his presence.

My bare feet hit the cold floor. One peek—*just one*—out the window.

The steam from Mrs. Allsopp's kitchen collected in this room—this small room—causing deposits to form on the panes. Seeing out was like looking through damp feathers. That, and the added frost, made spying difficult. But he *was* there, in the torch-lit alley, his shadow bleeding onto the snow.

It'd been three years since I'd seen this horseman. *The* Horseman. And, as then, his hand reached out, summoning me to him. *Katrina.*

A chill deeper than the winter cold embraced me and I wore it like a second skin.

Three times he's appeared since Ichabod and I fled to Philadelphia.

Why here? Why now?

Why me?

But whatever the reason, he wanted me—a want so strong, I was weak to resist.

Where will he take me?

His gloved fingers summoned me like willows waving in a breeze.

Katrina.

He sat proud in the saddle, his shoulders broad—an obsidian hole where his head should rest. Snapping back his cape, he tilted his hand that I might easily take it. How freeing it would be to throw myself onto the back of his horse and let him whisk me away.

He waited…wanted.

Katrina.

"What's out there?" The voice startled me, causing me to whip around. Violet, the girl I shared the room with above Allsopp's Pie Shop, sat up, her silhouette resembling a keyhole in the dark.

"Nothing," I answered. It was true. For when I turned back, he was gone.

She rustled the covers, lying back down. "Sleepwalkin' agin?"

"Yes." It was my best excuse.

I stole one last glimpse out the window, knowing tomorrow it would only be a dream—a ghost lingering in my weary mind.

I crawled under the covers, gooseflesh prickling my skin. Though a vast distance divided us, Sleepy Hollow would forever haunt me.

* * *

Mrs. Allsopp slapped another eel onto the butcher block. "Hurry, hurry, hurry."

I promptly severed its head and scored enough of the flesh to clamp it with the grippers. In four even tugs, I skinned it raw.

She dropped the head, along with others, into a pot for simmering. "Jane, hand me the salt."

Jane. My new name. It still felt as limp and cold as this eel. But a necessity. Katrina Van Tassel left Sleepy Hollow a wanted criminal. Jane Hanover entered Philadelphia a nobody. No skills. No kin. No prospects.

I had skills of course, bookkeeping, farm management, teaching. But without references, I might as well have been a guttersnipe groveling for food.

I gave Mrs. Allsopp the salt cellar. She worked me to the bone, but paid me with room and board—the room I shared with Violet, an Irish immigrant who was presently punching a lump of pie dough like it had somehow offended her.

The back door opened, bringing a burst of crisp air into the already warming kitchen. Seth, the youngest of Mrs. Allsopp's two sons, tromped in. *Speaking of eels.* Late, as usual. I'd never been to the Allsopp's home, but I could imagine Seth heaped up on a fine feather bed, not willing to rise till the last minute. He held a stringer with three hares.

"There're not dressed," I said, tossing him a sullen gaze.

He swung them toward me. "That's what Ma pays you for."

Well, she doesn't exactly *pay* me. But there are worse jobs than working in Mrs. Allsopp's pie shop.

Violet picked bits of pie dough from her knuckles. "I'll do it." She jerked the hares from his hand, her eyes glaring into his. At sixteen, she was two years younger than me, but a tall girl. And skilled at using her height to intimidate.

He backed away, grinning.

"Out of the kitchen, Seth," Mrs. Allsopp said, bumping him aside with her plump hip. "I'll call you when the pies are done."

He walked back to the door, but instead of exiting, as I had greatly hoped, he leaned against it, crossing his arms.

Seth was the only one of her sons who worked for her. His skill as a pie juggler kept her business afloat. Yes, a pie juggler. While she had a fair number of customers dine inside, mostly transients, Seth would load small pies onto a cart and move from block to block, juggling them like a vagabond street performer. It was quite amazing to watch. Not one pie ever met the dirt. And for whatever reason, people greatly desired a meal that, moments before, had been suspended in air. Seth felt that this unique talent put him above helping in the shop—though he had, until today, dressed the hares he'd brought for pie filling.

I continued my present task of chopping eels, stopping frequently to yawn.

"Will you stop all that yawning?" Mrs. Allsopp said, her mouth stretching into a wide O. "It's contagious."

Violet gripped a hare and pulled its hide like someone removing a pair of trousers from a doll. "Jane was sleepwalkin' again."

Mrs. Allsopp, stirring the fish stock, shook her head. "Oh, Jane, don't let the devil into your dreams. He'll lead you to no good."

But I had let him in. Three times now.

Seth grabbed up a paring knife and picked at some filth under his nails. "What Jane needs is a husband. One who'll see to it she goes to sleep content."

I couldn't argue with that, though he was implying himself, not the one person who could actually accomplish that task. The thought of bedding with Seth made the hairs on my neck bristle.

"Jane's usually a sound sleeper," Violet said. "Not a peep out've her."

Thank God. Had I talked in my sleep, Violet would've gotten an earful.

"And what are you dreaming about on the nights the devil don't come?" Seth asked, carving some curling grit from under his thumb nail.

Those nights were just as bad, though the nightmares I'd first suffered when first coming here were lessening. My only

8

peace of mind came once a week. The one the night I spent with Ichabod. *Tonight.*

"Ah, Jane." He pointed the knife toward me, circling it. "Your face went all buttery there for a moment."

"Only because I was stifling a yawn."

He cocked an eyebrow. "Those sweet dreams could come true, you know."

Violet chopped the head off another hare. "And I s'pose ya think you're the one who could make that happen?"

His face split into an ugly grin. "These hands can do more than juggle."

Oh God! I felt an urgent need to punch the pie dough.

Lucky for us, Mrs. Allsopp intervened. "Off with you, Seth." She flicked a pinch of salt at him. "These girls can work faster without all your flirting."

Only a mother would mistake that vulgarity for flirting.

"All right." He tromped toward the dining area, but stopped long enough to drop a large eel onto the butcher block. He pulled it taut and whispered, "This fellow's got nothing on me."

In one swift stroke, I brought the knife down, chopping it in two.

Seth's face stormed for a moment, then he bellowed a laugh and walked out.

* * *

At about two o'clock, Mrs. Allsopp handed me a pie wrapped in a heated cloth. "Jane, dear, would you take this over to Jonas?"

"Oh." Jonas…her other son. The polite one. He'd come into the shop on occasion, but this was the first time I'd been asked to deliver his meal. "He doesn't get his pies from Seth?"

Mrs. Allsopp flapped a hand as though waving it off. "Oh, you know Seth."

Unfortunately.

"He sometimes forgets to deliver."

Forgets? Ha. Their brotherly bickering could make the papers.

I glanced down at the bundled pie, my heartbeat stepping up. Going out risked exposure. *Is today the day I'd be discovered?* I tried to hand it back. "Mrs. Allsopp, I have an odd pain in my knee. I probably shouldn't walk too much. Can't Violet take it instead?"

She dismissed that too, in an oddly suspicious manner. "No, no. I need Violet here." Her tone suggested there would be no further discussion.

I wound my woolen cloak around me and went out the front door, into the crowded street.

Philadelphia had far exceeded my expectations. Row after row of brick buildings, stately homes, towering gothic churches, mansions, shops, and, of course, the seat of the

American government. Had I come here under different circumstances I would've reveled in the wonders of it. But I came here under desperate circumstances. So I kept my cowl low and my pace quick, thinking every face I encountered might be a possible pursuer from my past. Fear of recognition stalked me like a shadow.

Being a Saturday, High Street Market bustled. That was the day the farmers came to sell their meat and winter vegetables. I walked by Seth, pausing beyond the pocket of people he'd amassed. Mouths awed and eyes bloomed as four pies sailed crisscross over his cocked head. One by one, he caught them with a tray. All but one. Striking a pose with bent knee, he let the last land soundly upon the sole of his upturned shoe. *Ugh. Who's going eat that one?* His audience burst into applause.

I found I was holding my breath, hoping for once it'd land, top down, splat on his arrogant face.

Shame on me.

When the onlookers pushed forward, I scurried away.

Threading through the market crowds, I made my way to Thatcher and Son, Clockmakers. As fate would have it, Mr. Thatcher's son had died of yellow fever early last year. Soon after that, Thatcher hired Jonas to help with repairs. A sound, noble profession. No theatrics.

I opened the door to the cadence of ticking clocks and swinging pendulums. *Amazing!* Every wall was an exhibit of timepieces. I glided past shelves and tables of compasses, barometers, astrolabes and other navigational devices, fighting the urge to stop and examine each and every one.

Mr. Thatcher stood behind a counter, waiting on an elderly gentleman who appeared as weathered and worn as the pocket watch he dangled from his hand. They both looked toward me.

"Mrs. Allsopp asked me to deliver this to Jonas." I pulled back the cloth to show Mr. Thatcher the golden pie adorned with a goose pattern.

He broke into a smile and winked. "Where's mine?"

I liked him right away. "I'd be happy to fetch one for you. Seth Allsopp was juggling a few just two blocks over."

He patted his belly and sighed. "I'm teasing, my dear. Only an hour ago I had my fill of hot stew at the City Tavern." He reached back and opened a heavy red curtain. "You'll find Jonas in the back."

"Thank you."

I passed behind the counter and through the opening into a work area filled with disassembled clocks and other machinery. Jonas sat on a tall stool, looking boyish and casual, his white linen shirt opened to the gully of his throat. He focused intently, chewing his outer lip as he screwed a cog into the back of a polished brass clock. A lock of his sandy hair had escaped his queue and feathered against his cheek. As I drew near, he looked up, his amber eyes brightening. "Jane." He hopped up from his seat.

It was hard to believe this handsome young man with his gentle temperament and polite manners was any relation to Seth. I'd swear that juggling monkey had been left on their doorstep.

I held up the pie. "Your mother worries about your appetite." I then searched the table for an empty spot to place it. Seeing my dilemma, Jonas took the pie from me.

"She worries too much," he said, his smile tight. He shoved some repair work aside and set the pie down.

I stood, stupidly, staring at it, thinking I should make polite conversation. But say what? *It must get awfully noisy around here on the hour.* Or: *How long does it take to wind all these clocks each evening?* Instead I blurted, "I should hurry back. Enjoy your meal." I ran the words together so fast, it sounded like I was making for a quick escape. Which, of course, I was.

"Jane." He scratched the back of his head as though trying to find the courage to keep talking. "Stay for a few minutes. Keep me company while I eat."

Uh-oh. How do I politely refuse my employer's nice son? "I think Mrs. Allsopp is expecting me to return right away."

He removed some broken clockwork from a chair and offered me a seat. "I'll tell Mother you were detained on my account."

I hesitated a moment, then gently sat on the chair's edge. I'd spoken to Jonas on many occasions, but each time in the pie shop, amid other people. Usually our conversations were restricted to things like the weather, the rising cost of sugar, and political affairs of the State House. Should I worry this day's conversation would become more than that?

Instead of digging into the pie, he turned it slowly in a circle. I could practically see the inner workings of his thoughts.

A moment of panic seized me. *Am I about to be dismissed? Had Mrs. Allsopp instructed him to do her dirty work?*

Then, without taking his eyes off the pie, he asked, "Are you thinking of leaving us?"

What? My jaw came momentarily unhinged. "Leave?"

"Yes. The pie shop. Are you planning to leave? It's been three months and you still seem…uncomfortable."

Uncomfortable…yes. But it had nothing to do with my surroundings and everything to do with the events of my past. Three months could not erase all the horrors I'd witnessed.

"Is that why your mother sent me here? To discuss the state of my employment?"

He faltered, accidentally puncturing the pie with this finger. "No, no. It's not that at all. It's just that…"

I was naturally on my guard, frightened even. What would I do if I lost this position? "Just what?"

He huffed a breath as he pick up a rag and wiped the goose gravy from his hand. "It's always been evident that you've come from a different class of society."

"Evident?"

He sat back, studying me. "The way you speak. The way you carry yourself. When you're not hiding behind your apron, you converse on subjects most women your age yawn at."

I slumped a little, never realizing my carriage could reveal my privileged past. Perhaps I should be more like Violet. She skins eels and hares like it's an honor.

"And," he continued, "Mother told me as of late, you've been correcting the cost ledger."

I was only showing her how she could economize—"

"See!" He pointed a finger at me, causing me to start.

I placed a hand to my chest, my heart thumping.

"That's what I mean. I've never met another woman who uses words like 'economize.'"

Rot! Would I now have to watch every word out of my mouth? "Look, I won't lie to you. If I were able to better myself, I would. But baking pies is all I'm skilled to do." God strike me.

He nodded and sat back, still not attempting a single bite of the pie. I suspected he'd already eaten too. Probably some of that hot stew from the City Tavern. He picked up a rather large wind-up key and worried it between his fingers. "Truly, Jane, I am sorry we can't pay you above room and board. You work exceptionally hard."

Having seen the books, I knew the shop only brought in a modest sum. And barely enough for the Allsopp family. It was no secret that Mr. Allsopp, also taken by the fever, left them with a sizable debt. And with a debtors' prison just blocks away, it's a wonder they hadn't found themselves there.

"I've never asked for money," I said. "And I promise I never will. You provide what I need."

He stuttered a laugh. "I hardly think that." His eyes turned to me. "But I do want you to be happy."

Happy? My father had been recently murdered, my family home ravaged, three childhood friends had committed a crime that brought a plague upon our village, and my closest friend had treated me like the filth on the bottom of her shoe. Oh yes…and there was also that issue of having a price on my head. The only happiness here was the too few moments I spent with Ichabod.

"Jonas, I have learned that the world can be a cruel place. But you and your mother have shown nothing but kindness to me. Maybe one day I will be happy. But, for now, I'm content."

He kept his eyes on me, testing my sincerity. After some consideration, he nodded.

Feeling there was nothing left to say, I stood. I think that caught him off guard because when he popped up from his stool, his hand swept against a box of saw-toothed gears. He grasped for it, but too late. The box fell from the table, spilling a dozen or so tiny wheels to the floor. They plinked and scattered at our feet. His face flushed a deep scarlet as he gazed at the mess.

"Let me help you," I said, kneeling and picking up the box.

"Jane, no." I didn't think it was possible, but his face went even redder. He dropped to his knees nearly as quickly as the fallen box.

"It's no bother, really." With a teasing smile, I added, "After all, what would Mr. Thatcher say if he saw that his apprentice had strewn his inventory about?"

"He would probably say they'd be easier to retrieve with a broom."

"But that would take away all the adventure."

Though tedious, we plucked up the small flat pieces and dropped them back into the box.

"Jane," he whispered, when there were only a few gears left to retrieve, "clock making is a fine profession, but like you, I'm only content. I don't intend to do this forever."

He was intimately close. Too close. *Why was he confiding in me?* "But Mr. Thatcher has lost his only kin. You could inherit this shop one day."

He placed a finger to his lips as though I'd spoken too loudly. Then, lowering his voice even more, he said, "I realize. But it's not timepieces that interest me."

There was a boyish glint behind his eyes that put me at ease. "No?"

He stood and offered his hand, helping me to rise. "I want to show you something."

We crossed to a back corner table that held a large case covered with a rich-blue velvet cloth. "This is what I work on in the evenings when the shop is closed. I've only shown it to a few." He unveiled the case and sprang a latch that allowed the sides to open out.

Oh! I drew my hand to my mouth, practically speechless. "Jonas…" Before me was a magnificent clockwork doll wearing ivory satin breeches and tailcoat. He was seated behind a small glass armonica. Most of the inner workings of his body was exposed, but I was sure that in time the entire thing would be complete.

"Watch," Jonas said, pride lacing his words. Using a long narrow key, he reached through a slit in the back of the doll's clothing and clicked one of the mechanisms. With the twist of another, the figure sprang to life. Its soft leather fingers touched the glass and a beautiful baroque piece began to play.

"Pachelbel's Canon in D," I said, still awed at the precision of the machine.

Jonas waggled a finger at me. "Ah-ha. The mysterious Jane reveals even more of her past."

Something I had not intended to do.

"Honestly, Jonas, I'm at a loss for words. You built this completely on your own?"

He raised an eyebrow as a smile ghosted his lips. "My brother is not the only talented Allsopp."

"Indeed he is not."

* * *

The room Violet and I shared was not much bigger than a horse stall...about as comfortable as well. The chill from the Delaware River seeped in, and the walls wore it like a fresh coat of paint.

Violet sat on the end of our small bed, fastening a shirt hook as I braided her copper hair.

"Will you stay still?" I asked her. "I'm almost done."

19

She ignored me, fastening the next. "Men have it so much easier than us."

"You're just now discovering that?" Good heavens, she had a lot to learn.

"I mean their clothes. Far more comfortable and very little to lace."

"These being a size too big is what makes them agreeable. I would think a man's breeches would be confining and awkward for sitting."

She bounced up and down, tugging at a leg of the ones she wore. "I rather like 'em."

"Be still."

No, Violet didn't always dress in men's clothing. This was how Ichabod and I managed to spend one night a week together—he and Violet trading places. She, getting to curl up in his soft bed at the men-only boarding house. Me, getting to curl up next to him. Right after coming here he'd secured a position as an apprentice at a law firm. The pay was poor and the hours endless, but it afforded him a decent room. What it did not afford was the opportunity for us to marry. Not until he received a law degree. It was the perfect career choice for him, but how many Saturdays could we risk?

I made another attempt to tie off her braid, careful not to touch the roping scars that descended down her back. She took great pains to hide them while dressing, so I never asked how they came to be there. Most likely the results of a cruel father or uncle back in Dublin. She held her past locked away as I did mine.

"I've grown to love pipe tobacco too," she added.

"Violet! Please tell me you haven't taken up smoking a pipe." The thought curdled my stomach.

"Nay," she said, giggly. "I love inhalin' the sweet aroma as the men at the boardin' house gather for brandy, smokin', and cards. I've peeked out to watch."

"You've peeked out? Violet, no."

"Don't worry. I'm never caught."

"So far." I couldn't bear the consequences if our ruse was discovered.

I tucked her braid into the collar of the shirt. She rose and slipped on the plum-colored waistcoat.

"Just remember what you'd be giving up if you were found out," I reminded. "One night a week in a warm comfortable bed. All to yourself. No more soft blankets, plump pillows, or—"

"Pipe tobacco." She set about buttoning herself in. "I'm well aware." She glimpsed me through the corners of her eyes and her lips curved into a smile. "But I'm sure you're more worried about what *you'd* be givin' up."

I refused to think of it!

I hung my apron on the hook and took down my blue dress. I'd once had a wardrobe filled with exquisite silks, deep velvets and fine-spun lace. And days when my most pressing matter was deciding which hat and gloves to wear. At present, I owned two dresses. The ill-fitting gray one—rustic by any means—that I wore every day, and the homespun blue one I saved for this one special night of the week.

"I don't know why ya bother changin' yer dress," Violet said. "It comes off right after he arrives."

My jaw dropped and I gave her a teasing shove. "You don't know that."

She cast me another slantwise look, brow raised.

What could I say? She was right. Still, I went about dressing for Ichabod, while she went about dressing to resemble him. Bless her and her added height.

"Jane..."

I didn't like the hesitant tone in her voice. "Yes?"

"I was just thinkin' about Seth."

Oh, God take us! "And risk polluting your mind?" I thought that would bring a chuckle, but she continued bothering with her clothing.

"Is he really all that bad?"

I considered it, searching for a redeeming quality. "Well...he does have superb juggling skills."

More hesitation on her part as she busied herself with the already fluffed neckcloth .

I hated pursuing the topic of Seth, but I needed to know what was brewing in her head. "Why do you ask?"

"Never mind."

"But I do mind." The thought of her and Seth carrying on had me tasting bile.

She shrugged a little. "It's just that he invited me to a party."

That scoundrel! He'd badgered me about accompanying him to that party all week. Though I didn't think Violet needed to know that. "A party tonight?"

Her face grew long and doleful. "Yes."

Oh rot! What was I to say? If I'd continued my criticism, that Seth Allsopp was a loutish creature whose career depended on his mother's baking skills, she'd have thought I was only saying it to keep her to our agreement. I gestured toward her clothes. "You obviously turned him down."

"Of course. I know how much tonight means to ya. And who am I to stand in the way of true love?"

But am I standing in her way? "Believe me, you could do far better than Seth. What about his brother Jonas? He's quite handsome." There could be a match there.

Her face pinched like I'd suggested she shovel manure. "He's too old."

He was Ichabod's age.

"Honestly, Violet, would you want to end up with someone like Seth?"

"Nay. But I would love to go to a party."

I paused my undressing and cast a look her way. "If you really want to go…"

Thankfully, she waved it off. "Nah. I'm guessin' any party Seth is invited to is probably no place for decent folk."

A good point.

Once my blue dress was secured, I pinned my hair, pinched my cheeks, and double-checked myself in the hand mirror, making sure all flour and pie flakes had been scrubbed away.

"You look so beautiful, Jane."

Beautiful? She should have seen me before creases formed at my lips and dark circles settled under my eyes. "Thank you."

As always, my heart beat along with the seconds, waiting for Ichabod's arrival. As the tower clock struck nine, Violet met him at the back door and led him up to our room. One glance at his gorgeous face and vibrant green eyes was enough to set my soul afire. And his smile could erase every moment of weariness I'd endured.

He looked me up and down as though I were a sanctuary. "Jane." The name always sounded hollow on his

24

tongue. He then turned to Violet. "And a good evening to my counterpart."

Her eyes twinkled like evening stars. "Good evenin', Mr. Zachary Crane."

Zachary Crane. Though there was no price on his head, he could still be sought for abetting. But he felt it safe to go by his middle name, not wanting to practice law under an alias. I was thankful. Posing as someone else was a life for lawbreakers...like me.

Violet held out her hand for Ichabod's heavy coat. He slipped it off and helped her on with it. "You know, one day I will greatly reward you for this."

Her cheeks dimpled. "You say that all the time. My reward is gettin' to stretch out on a bed that me feet don't dangle off." She reached out, grabbed his hat and cocked it on her head. "'Course, the real reward is how agreeable Jane is after you've come to visit."

"Violet! I'm always agreeable."

She grinned at Ichabod and winked. "But not always smilin'."

Never smiling...*except now*. Oh...I saw her point.

"All right then, I'll step to," she said.

"Wait," He turned her around and reached into the coat pocket, withdrawing a small leather-bound book trimmed in gold. Ichabod had become my personal librarian. Every

Saturday he'd loan me a different book from his employer's library. And from what he'd described, the selection was vast.

Anxious, I took it from him.

"What's it say?" Violet asked, peering at the cover. She was making progress in the reading lessons I provided her, but this title was beyond her capabilities.

I read: "*A Vindication of the Rights of Woman: with Strictures on Political and Moral Subjects* by Mary Wollstonecraft." Ichabod knew me too well.

Her eyes widened. "Well, that's a fancy lot o' words."

Yes, and I look forward to reading every one.

She loped to the door, but before walking out, she turned and waggled a finger at me. "Don't ya be sleepwalkin' now."

Ichabod whipped around, a trio of creases upon his brow. "Sleepwalking?"

I waved it off. "It's nothing." The last thing I wanted was to ruin my evening with talk of a headless horseman, gruesome nightmares, and my ties to the past. Those were best grieved alone.

He looked at Violet, an eyebrow high in question.

She shrugged, knowing she'd said too much. "Jane just gets restless, that's all."

True. *Definitely* true.

"Nothin' to worry over," she added. "G'night." With that, she bounded down the stairs.

Ichabod gently closed the door. In two seconds I was in his arms. His touch could wash away every pent-up worry. "Katrina." It was as though my name had been trapped inside him and he could no longer contain it. He immediately brought his lips to mine, consuming me. He then lay kisses on my jaw, my earlobe and down my neck, bringing forth the fire and passion I kept hidden all week.

"Katrina," he whispered, another reminder that the real me was not entirely lost.

I eagerly fumbled with the buttons on his waistcoat as his hand went behind me, unfastening my dress. Yes, as Violet said, that dress was soon off and cast aside.

He eased me onto the bed—our kisses eager and impassioned. My flesh ached for this. *Why can't I have him here every night?*

I became lost in the lovemaking, his splendid body fitting so perfectly to mine. I put all else aside. No world existed outside this tiny candlelit room.

Afterward, he cradled my body to his, our breathing quick and uneven. Then, placing a tender kiss upon my temple, he whispered, "I love you."

I gazed up at him, wanting to see as well as hear it. "I love you too."

I lay my head against his shoulder, melting into his embrace.

He gently stroked my cheek. "Sleepwalking?"

Ahhhh! He had enough worry on his shoulders. I wouldn't burden him with this. "As I said, it's nothing."

"Are the nightmares back?" I couldn't fool him.

They've never gone. "Not like they were before."

The couple of weeks after escaping, I remained restless and prone to panic. Each second of slumber was a nightmare trapped within itself. In sleep, I relived the horror of Sleepy Hollow—the beheadings, my ghastly attack upon the jailor, and endured constant dreams of being recaptured and hanged.

Ichabod held me. "If only I could be with you every night."

If only.

We both knew it wasn't safe to be together. Not with this price on my head.

I laid a gentle kiss on his neck. "Don't worry so much. Violet is here with me. Concentrate on your career instead. Maybe soon you can find a loophole—a way to free me for good."

"Believe me if there is a way, I will find it."

If there is a way.

These desperate promises always followed our lovemaking. Time to move on. I nuzzled my face against him. "So tell me about your week."

"Cordwainers." His sigh practically raised the quilt.

I drew back, studying his face in the dim candlelight. "Cordwainers?"

"There is a labor dispute brewing among the Federal Society of Journeymen Cordwainers. The shoemakers are insisting on stable pay and have called for a turn-out." He looked upon me, his eyes dim. "Of course you know what that means."

"That there will be a shortage of shoes?"

He laughed a little. "Not yet. But the urgency has added even more tasks to the ones Mr. Hammond expects to perform."

"But what about your pursuits? Aren't you studying the law material?"

"I've barely had time to read anything above the pile of documents I'm given to copy. And I'm getting no more than a few hours' sleep each night." He wiggled his wrist. "My right hand may become arthritic before my next birthday."

I took it and brought it to my lips for a soft kiss. "Hmmm…it was functioning properly just moments ago."

A devilish smile curled his lips. "You have a talent for bringing new life to all parts of me."

"Oh really? Would you like to put that theory to test once again?" I pulled him in for a long luscious kiss. His heartbeat quickened as he held me close.

I loved him more than anything. And I loved how he loved me...in every aspect. But was that love for me a drawback? He didn't deserve to be a copy clerk, or, in his case, a common servant to the firm. This brilliant man would not only be a fine lawyer, but could one day be seated in the State House as well. I could see a bright political future for him. Yet I knew of no politicians' wives wanted for murder.

All these years, I'd taken my father's wealth for granted. Now I'd give anything for just a tenth of his worth. But after Father's murder, the house had been ravaged—all he'd worked for gone. How stupid I'd been. There *were* still riches to be had back there, but I dared not risk my neck to retrieve them.

"I will make things right," I murmured.

It wasn't until Ichabod ceased his tender kisses that I realized I'd spoken it aloud. "We both will," he whispered against my ear. "In time."

Yes. *In time.*

* * *

As always, morning came long before I was ready. My upbringing had me in church every Sunday. No more. I'd left my faith back in the Hollow along with everything else. And believe me I'd burn in hell before giving up my precious time with Ichabod.

Too soon, Violet was back with Ichabod's coat and hat. And after several clinging kisses, he left, leaving me and my aching heart for another agonizing week.

But an afternoon sun appeared, turning the dismal day into a longing to venture out. Unfortunately, that meant others would be out too. More people than I cared to encounter. But I couldn't bear another moment penned inside. I swept on my cloak, pulling the cowl low over my face. Then, stretching on my gloves, I turned to Violet. "Coming with me?"

She plucked her ragged pelisse from the peg and grinned. "Don't I always?"

We each took an apple from the kitchen before making our exit from the pie shop.

The cherished sunlight did little to heat the frigid air. We made the cold walk, rustling through the back streets, to a home on the outskirts of the city. The estate was small, several acres with a stables in the back. Violet and I, careful not to be seen, veered around to it. The owner had four horses at pasture—one a red roan with an extra bushy tail. This horse, lovingly named Dewdrop, once belonged to me. Seeing her always filled a hollow spot in my heart.

When Ichabod and I arrived in early November, the first thing he did was sell our horses—the only thing of value we owned. That bought us three-week's lodging in one of the waterfront taverns, as well as a welcomed change of clothes. My only attire until then was the dress I'd escaped in, worn inside-out to hide the blood and filth. My body and mind had been numb of all feeling, and parting with my beloved horse was yet another goodbye. But I could sneak an occasional visit. Much like my time with Ichabod.

Violet and I leaned against the hoar-rimed railing. I held the apple out and called, "Dewdrop."

She galloped straight to me, tail high.

"Sunshine!" Violet called to a palomino that she favored. She had no way of knowing that Dewdrop had once been mine. She thought the name was something I conjured for a strange horse I'd taken a particular liking to. The palomino, of course, was not as cooperative. It traipsed and dilly-dallied for a time, never looked our way.

Dewdrop butted her muzzle against my cheek and took the apple. I reached out and stroked her smooth strong neck. How I longed to saddle and ride her.

After calling the palomino two more times, Violet slumped. She switched her gaze to the house and chewed at her bottom lip. "I wonder what it's like to have a home like that."

It was half the size of the Van Tassel mansion, which of course now stood in shambles.

I shrugged like it was beyond me. "I hope to one day know." I hoped for a lot of things.

Violet rolled her apple between her palms. "No doubt ya will when Zachary's a fancy attorney."

"That could be ages." *If ever.*

"He's the smartest gent I ever met. You should see that lot of books in his room."

I'd give anything.

"Some of 'em have words 'bout as long as me pinkie." She stretched one of hers out for emphasis. "Any word that long must mean somethin' real important."

"Violet, the size of the word isn't necessarily connected to its meaning."

"But the way I figure it, if Zachary can read those fancy words, he'll be somebody special someday."

"He's already special."

"I mean he'll be a respected member of *real* society." She poked me with her finger. "And you'll be the lady right there by 'im."

I wished I could see that future, the one she so zealously imagined.

"And in them days," she added, "I could come work for ya, as yer kitchen maid or such."

"Oh, Violet, what makes you think you won't also marry well?"

She took a bite of the apple and spoke as she chewed. "You're a funny one, Jane. You know men don't fancy tall gawky girls with no schoolin'. Unless me wealth matched me height, I s'pose."

"Absurd. I'm teaching you to read. We'll work on your grammar as well. No one need ever know of your life back in Dublin."

She grew still and held the apple like that one bite had soured. How I wish I could ask her what had transpired there. But she was as secretive about her life as I was with mine.

After a moment, she recovered. "By the time I've learnt to read and talk like a lady, I'll be a haggard old maid."

"Fine then," I said, teasing. "But the lessons will continue, even when you're in my employ"—I poked her back—"ironing my monogrammed towels."

Her adorable smile reflected in her eyes.

"Though," I continued, "I still feel you'll find a suitable husband by then."

"Not stuck in Mrs. Allsopp's kitchen, I won't. The only man I ever see is Seth. And Jonas on occasion."

"You're only sixteen. Some handsome, *respectable* young man will appear." Though she was right. She spent all of her time in the kitchen or in our room. *No wonder she loves dressing up like Ichabod and sneaking out.*

As though reading my mind, she said, "There is a man at the boardin' house who has the room across from Zachary's. I only just noticed him so I think he's new."

Please, no! "Violet, you worry me. You should be staying locked in Zachary's room."

Her eyes bloomed wide. "Oh no. He don't see me. I watch 'im through the keyhole. He keeps his door open, makin' it easy."

"Still."

But her gaze was back on the palomino and her mind on the new tenant. "He's quite handsome. And he has this wonderful way of snappin' his coattails when he sits down at the desk by his bed. I watch while he writes letters." She cocked her head, her brows dipping. "I wish I knew who he was writin' to."

"Don't get too love struck. Those letters could be to a wife."

"Ah, but he's so elegant."

I'd never seen anyone so dreamy-eyed. "So you think the snapping of tails makes him elegant?"

"Not just that. It's his fancy clothes and polished boots. He's a fine figure of a man. Almost as handsome as Zachary."

"Then maybe I should ask Zachary about him," I said, playing to her fantasies. "Who knows? Maybe he could become a suitor."

Her mouth split into a broad grin. "There ya go agin, Jane. He's too fine a fella for me. But I do love the mystery of 'im."

It was her love of mystery that scared me most. It took ages for her to stop asking about my past—she who revealed little of her own. But I fed her the same lie I'd told the Allsopps. I came here from Vermont after a fire had taken everything and everyone. Poor devastated Jane could barely speak of it.

"I'll ask Zachary if he's made his acquaintance. Maybe he can shed some light on your mystery man."

Dewdrop snorted, bobbing her head near Violet—wanting her apple. Since Violet couldn't coax "Sunshine," she lifted it to the horse's mouth. That's when I heard several light footsteps crunching on the icy ground. A riding crop cracked against Dewdrop's hindquarters, sending her galloping off. A wiry man with narrowed eyes filled the vacant space. His lips were pursed, his cheeks wine-colored, and he had a giant mole near his nose that sprouted more hair than his chin. He gripped the whip like he might use it on us.

I took a few steps back, but Violet stumbled and cowered behind me. Silly, considering she'd have to squat for me to hide her six-foot frame.

The man stepped up to the fence, his pupils pinpoints. "You got no business with these horses."

Judging by his weathered clothes, he was neither the owner of the home or the stock. *Definitely in the master's employ.*

"I'm sorry," I said. "We didn't mean any harm. We just enjoy watching them."

He picked up the apple that Violet dropped in her panic. "I take care of these nags. I feed them. Me. Nobody else."

And beat them daily with that crop? "I understand."

"Then get gone or I'll alert the authorities!"

I reached back and gripped Violet's wrist. "No need. We're leaving."

His face stayed screwed in a grimace as I hooked my arm through Violet's and escorted her away.

We barely spoke as we scuttled back to the shop, my mind on Dewdrop and the hole in my heart. Could I keep nothing from my prior life?

* * *

My past caught up to me once again, invading my sleep. I dreamt of Marten, a dear friend who'd sought to rescue me from my stale existence within my father's domain.

Marten drops the supplies from his arms as he gapes at his ship—practically on its side, battered and partly run ashore. Marked by a vengeful Horseman.

My clothes, soaked through, cling to my skin and the bitter cold burns my flesh. Every inch of my weary body aches.

A second, maybe two. Then...

37

Hooves thundering. The smell of cinder in the air. He appears.

Look at his shoes, Katrina, look at his shoes. *But I see only a headless figure and the glint of his scythe.*

"Oh God, Marten, run! Run!"

Why does he not obey? Why does he not flee?

Marten turns, throwing his arm up to shield his face. The scythe slashes him like a hot blade through butter. Blood spews. Droplets dance above his body before it falls. His head rolls toward me like a rock tumbling down a hill.

"No! No! No!"

I stagger back, though not fast enough. The head comes to a stop at my feet, his face contorted in terror, his slayer's image now imprinted on his crystalline blue eyes.

The Horseman approaches—

I stumble back into the freezing waters of the Hudson. "I sent you away! I sent you away!"

No. Not him. Not this *Horseman.*

I know this, yet my mind is still muddled. I sent you away!

I bolted straight up from sleep, my heart a clapper in my chest. The pull, like an ox dragging a plow, had me on my feet. I padded to the window, knowing he'd be there.

I sent you away.

It had only been two days. Just two. Why was he back so soon?

I pressed my hands to the rimy pane and leaned my forehead against it. *Just go to him, Katrina. Let him take you.*

He opened his cape and extended his arm, lifting it toward me. The summoning was so strong I wanted to dive through the glass. I clenched my fist and gritted my teeth. *No. I will not come.*

He closed his fingers into a fist and drew his hand back, pulling the invisible cord that bound us.

"No, no, no," I murmured. Enough. Enough! *I sent you away!*

Hitching my nightdress, I swept out the door and down the narrow stairs. The dark kitchen was a maze of shadows, but I maneuvered it without light. I rounded past the pantry, the butcher blocks and counter, to the stone hearth on the far wall. Snatching up the fire poker, I sailed to the door. Not a practical weapon of course, but my brain was mired with anger and fatigue.

I rushed through the door, into the alley, poker high above my head. I half expected he'd have vanished, but he still sat astride his great steed, patient as any ghost, I imagine.

Like a madwoman, I charged, swinging the iron rod. "Begone, devil!" I brought it down hard, connecting with the horse's rump. The horse snorted, billowing smoke from its nostrils. Or maybe it was winter vapor. My rapid breath hung before me too.

As I raised the poker again, the Horseman snatched it from my grasp. In one swift move, he flung it. It spun through the air and stuck like a dagger into the door.

My fury outweighed my fear, and I refused to back down. "Go away!"

In a blink, he unsheathed his sword and pressed the tip to the soft palate under my chin. Its stinging prick was the first real sensation I'd felt in weeks. That, and the warm trickle of blood inching down my neck.

I stood as still as the buildings surrounding me, my breathing shallow and quick. Facing off with a man who had none. I then closed my eyes, covering them with my hands. Seconds ticked away, the sword still piercing my skin.

"If you want me," I said, "you'll have to take me. Or kill me. But I will not willingly come."

More seconds passed as I stood in that freezing alley. By day, it was filled with delivery carts, cooing pigeons, and stray dogs. Tonight, it was just me, in my thin nightdress, my bare feet frozen to the ground.

"Take me or kill me," I repeated.

A hand swooped down, clasping my shoulder. I sucked in a quick breath.

"Jane!" Violet twirled me into tight hug. "Girl, yer sleepwalkin' agin."

I opened my eyes and turned my head. Only the empty alley lay before me.

"Come inside," she urged, "before ya catch a fever. And look"—she traced her finger along my neck and held it out—"You're bleedin'."

"Did you see him?" I whispered.

Her face dipped in worry. "Who?"

"Him," I repeated, tears moistening my eyes.

"I didn't see nobody. Now come along. You're scarin' me."

She led me back to the door, still open, but before going in, I looked on the other side. It took the two of us to remove the fire poker buried deep within it.

* * *

Violet started a fire, used the now bent poker to stir it, then put on a kettle. Thankfully, she didn't ask how the poker ended up embedded in the door. "Up you go," she said, ushering me to our room. She sat me on the end of the bed and wiped the dirt from my feet. After tightly winding the quilt around me, she took a look at the nick stinging my neck. "It's nothing serious." She dabbed at it with a clean spot on the rag.

Nothing serious? This had *not* been a dream. *Not now. Nor when I awake in the morning.*

I shifted my eyes to the window, but Violet squeezed my chin and redirected my gaze. She then plopped the clammy rag into my hand and raised it to the wound. A chill veined though me that took my breath. Waggling a finger, she said, "Now don't go wanderin' off while I'm fetchin' the tea."

Not to worry, Violet. I hadn't the strength to wander.

The moment she left, I tossed the rag into the corner and huddled deeper into the quilt. Why was the Horseman stalking me? What magic did he hold that pulled me to him? *He was there. I've not gone completely lunatic...yet.*

Violet soon returned with two steaming cups. I freed my arms from the quilt to take one.

She sat, hovering close, her own body trembling from the cold. "So tell me, Jane...why? What's causin' the sleepwalkin'?" She slurped a tiny sip of her tea.

I took a sip too, the hot drink easing a soreness in my throat. "I'm not sure," I lied. Then, with a slight shrug: "I've a destructive nature, I guess."

"Ah, Jane. I don't much know about such things as that, but I do know you've a kind and gentle heart."

"Ha! You *don't* know, Violet. You don't know anything about me." I turned toward her, the steam from her cup rising between us. "I could've done despicable things in my past."

Her eyes rounded. "What things?"

"Theft. Grave-robbing. Murder."

I expected her to go running into the night, but she didn't bat an eye. "You don't look like someone who'da done them things."

I traced a finger down her back, her wincing at my touch. "Unlike yours, my scars can't be seen."

She cowered, speaking softly. "Scars don't always make us what we are."

Don't they? "I'd like to believe that; I honestly would. But my *gentle* heart has been torn apart too many times. I've been a fool over and over, and everyone who's ever loved or trusted me has dearly paid."

She leaned, laying her cheek to my shoulder. "I love you and I haven't paid."

Dear sweet Violet. I tilted my head against hers. "Of course you have. I continually ask so much of you."

"But I get so much in return. And you're teachin' me to read. That's a fair trade. Just yesterday when I was clearin' off a table, there was a man next to me readin' a newspaper. And guess what? I was able to make out one of the headlines. Ya know what it said?"

"That there was a labor dispute among the cordwainers?"

She lifted her head and stared, her eyes practically crossed. "What?"

I waved it off, coming close to a smile. "Never mind. What'd it say?"

43

"It said, *Rats in Paris*."

Now my eyes crossed. "Rats in Paris?"

"That's what I made out."

Rats in Paris? How was that news? I wrapped my mind around it. My impoverished conditions had not stopped me from keeping up with the goings-on outside the shop. But rats in Paris? Then it hit me. *Riots in Paris!* I gave Violet an encouraging smile. "That's wonderful. I'm so proud of your progress."

"Me too," she said, grinning wide.

The tea and the quilt worked their magic as I was beginning to feel vital body parts again. "Maybe we should try and sleep now. Mrs. Allsopp won't like it if we're both yawning in the morning."

She set our cups on the tiny table by the door, then took great pains to tuck me in.

"You don't have to mother me, Violet."

She crawled in beside me, cuddling close. "I can't have ya gettin' sick now, can I? Who'd help me bake the pies?"

"That's true." Then raising a brow: "Maybe you could persuade Seth."

That brought a giggle. "Yeah, and maybe King George will discover I'm his long lost daughter and fetch me back to come live in his palace."

"Right. I'll wager the second."

I blew out the candle and we nestled together for warmth. Just as my eyes were closing, she said, "Jane, I'm sorry for whatever happened to you before."

I didn't deserve her. "Thank you, Violet. For everything."

* * *

On Wednesday morning Violet shook me awake. "I'm skinnin' the eels today. You dress the hares."

I sat up and stretched. Two nights free of *sleepwalking*. Thank goodness. Violet had threatened to tie my ankle to hers, but I reminded her how awkward that'd be should I get up to relieve myself. *A restful dreamless night. Had I scared the Horseman away for good?*

I crawled out of bed, dressed, and hurried out, leaving Violet pinning her hair. As I descended the stairs, I heard Jonas. I paused, stepped back and crouched, eavesdropping being one of my many devious talents.

His voice held a tremor. "Mother, you don't seem to be grasping the situation. The money is due at quarter's end. We're running out of options."

"Then speak to someone about an extension." Mrs. Allsopp rattled pans a bit louder than usual. I wasn't sure if she was trying to muffle his words or wake Violet and me to come to her rescue.

"It would be a wasted effort," he said. "Just, please, talk to Seth when he comes in. It's time he found real employment."

"And just who do you think would sell pies on the street, I might ask?"

"One of the girls could do that." The frustration in his tone was like an overwound clock. "They could take turns."

No, please. I thought. *Only Violet.* While I'd love a break from the shop, I couldn't risk exposure.

"They can't juggle!" she squawked. I could envision her cornflower-blue eyes popping wide.

"Oh, for God's sake, Mother, they don't need to juggle. People buy pies because they're hungry, not because they enjoy eating props from a theatrical display."

The pan rattling stopped. "But what else is he fit for?"

If I'd a coin for every time I'd asked myself that same question.

"He has a strong back," Jonas said. "There are plenty of jobs at the wharf. Mother, your shop is at stake. If they take it, we'll lose the house too."

I'm sure he had more to say, but at that moment Violet tromped up behind me. "What ya dilly-dallyin' for? Let's get goin'."

Both Jonas and Mrs. Allsopp quickly hushed as we descended. Jonas, dressed in a gray coat and blue vest, held tight to the ledger Mrs. Allsopp used to record deliveries and supplies.

I nodded to them as I walked in. "Good morning."

"Good morning," Jonas returned. He smiled at me like I was someone who could magically produce their much needed money. *If only.*

"Mornin'," Violet said, pushing by and accidentally knocking me against Jonas's arm. His face blushed the color of crushed roses. I could practically smell the awkwardness seeping from him.

Mrs. Allsopp went about tapping the flour sifter as if nothing were amiss. Yet I could see the worry creases etched deeper around her eyes. I wondered what bothered her most, losing the shop or telling Seth that he'd have to give up being a street performer and earn a real man's wage.

I slipped my apron on and readied the usual utensils. Jonas watched timidly. I sensed he had something to say, but not the nerve to say it. *Thank goodness.* Still, I couldn't pretend he wasn't in the room.

"I take it you are well, Jonas?"

He perked at my question. "As well as any person scraping by."

That opened the air for a suggestion. "That reminds me." I turned to Mrs. Allsopp. "I've been thinking perhaps we shouldn't salt the meat so much."

I might as well have suggested we torch the place. "Don't be silly," she said. "We can't have the meat going bad."

"But," I continued, "less salt would make it less dry. And tender meat produces more juice, more flavor. That could allow you to cut back on the amount you add to each pie. You could make up the difference with potatoes and carrots. None of your patrons would be the wiser and it would reduce costs."

She shook her head. "I don't know about that, Jane. If we start cutting corners, we'll surely start cutting customers."

"Mother," Jonas said, his voice even. "I think she's right. It's time we cut back. What she proposes is logical."

She sighed with a little extra flair. "All right, we'll try it." Then she cast me a playful snippety look. "Have you any more brilliant ideas to share?"

"I do," Violet squeaked, her eyes round and unsure.

We waited.

"Well, out with it," Mrs. Allsopp prodded.

Violet kept her gaze on the butcher block. "Stop storin' the potatoes so close to the onions."

We all stared, eager for an explanation. She looked like someone caught with her hand in the till. Finally she cast her eyes to Mrs. Allsopp. "It's just that the onions 'cause 'em to rot quicker."

Mrs. Allsopp threw up her hands, slinging a dust storm of flour. "Listen to you lot. After all these weeks you're suddenly all culinary experts."

"I don't know 'bout all that," Violet said, "but I know somethin' about onions and potatoes."

I bit back a smile.

"Anything else?" Mrs. Allsopp urged. "Spit it out now."

"Just one other suggestion," I dared.

Jonas had the look of Seth's gawkers, obviously quite amused.

Mrs. Allsopp crossed her chubby arms.

"Pork prices are low," I said. "Offer more pork than beef pies to the street patrons. Or maybe..." I glanced toward Violet and raised an eyebrow. "We could start selling sausages."

Violet cocked her head in serious thought. "You think Seth can sausage juggle?"

"I don't believe it!" Mrs. Allsopp yelled, her shout bouncing off the smoke-smudged ceiling. "Maybe I should just turn everything over to the two of you."

I chanced a look at Jonas. His gaze was on me. He still wore a smile, but his eyes were narrowed, suspicious. He placed a hand to his hip. "I have to admit, Jane, I'm impressed. How do you know so much about the price of pork?"

I couldn't risk discovery by explaining that hogs were easily fattened with inferior corn and didn't require the more expensive grain needed to produce beef. A simple lie would suffice. "I've seen the delivery bills." Not even a total lie.

He nodded, not looking convinced. "Very well." He went to Mrs. Allsopp, whose face was now a dark crimson. He bent and kissed one of her rosy cheeks. "Listen to these ladies, Mother. They make sense."

He gave us a slight bow as he took up his hat. "Jane. Violet. Have a nice day."

I acknowledged him with a nod.

Violet waved a floppy eel his way. "Bye, Jonas."

* * *

A good thirty minutes passed, the three of us bustling about the kitchen.

Mrs. Allsopp glanced at the clock. "I wonder where Seth is. I swear, that boy."

Just as she said it, the man himself appeared. His eyes were red-rimmed, his nose ruddy, and the odor of rum preceded him.

Mrs. Allsopp looked up from her stirring. "Where on God's green earth have you been all night?"

All night?

"What difference does it make, I'm here now." He hawked up a spit and shot it into the alley before slamming the door.

"Good then." She pointed to the extra dough on the counter. "You can help us get these pies in the oven quicker."

He plucked three lemons from a bowl and juggled them one-handed. I'd long stopped being impressed.

"Nah," he said, keeping his eyes on the flying fruit. "Too many cooks and all that. I'll bring the cart around when they're ready." As each lemon descended, he tapped it with his elbow, causing it to arc and plop back into the bowl. The man was insufferable. We could all find ourselves on the street and we'd have him to thank for it.

To test his sincerity, I paused from preparing crust and said, " Seth…" My saying his name suddenly brought life to his bloodshot eyes. He perked like a hunting dog. I continued, pretending not to notice. "Perhaps you could teach me to do that." Not that I had any real intention of selling pies on the street.

His lips curved upward and he let out a small chuckle. Then another, a little louder. He then fell into a fit of laughter. "You want *me* to teach *you* to juggle?"

I didn't share in his mirth. "Was I not clear?"

Violet turned, her face pleading. "Me too. You could teach us both."

He leaned against the table and crossed his arms, obviously quite pleased that two women were asking favors. "I don't know. That'd be a great risk on my part. You might become too good and Ma would never forgive me if her two cooks up and joined the circus." He let out another belly laugh that bristled the hairs on my arms.

I waited till he got his amusement under control. "I was thinking if there was another of us skilled at it, we could work different areas at the same time. Sell twice as many pies."

Mrs. Allsopp looked up, her face a bit brighter. "That's not such a bad idea, Seth."

Seth kept his gaze on me, his expression hard. "It's a god-awful idea. It'd take months for you to learn it, and we couldn't sell twice as many if you're out there dropping them on the ground...or worse, on the customers."

I wanted to slap that ridiculous grin that followed.

"We've got to do something soon," Mrs. Allsopp said, more to herself than to us.

I waited, wondering if she'd bring up Jonas's insistence that Seth take another job and leave the pie peddling to Violet and me. But she carried on as usual. Smart, really. This was not the time and place for a Seth tantrum. Who knew what he'd do when she finally approached him? My poor Ichabod worked ungodly hours and this man loafed about, relying on his mother, brother, and a few hours of juggling to get by.

52

One more miscarriage of fate. Didn't surprise me though. Not anymore.

"Maybe you can hire another girl," Seth told her.

Mrs. Allsopp's eyes sprung wide. "Have you gone mad? Where would I put her?" She pointed her chin our way. "These two can barely squeeze in that room upstairs."

He sauntered over and leaned against the sideboard where I stood. Taking the goose feather I was using for the egg wash, he traced it across my bottom lip and whispered, "There's plenty of extra room in my bed at home."

I snatched the feather back and quelled the impulse to ram it up his nose. "Don't be so quick to propose it, Seth. This new girl you want to hire could be far prettier than me."

He smiled, showing a chipped tooth. "Well then, we'd just have to work out a rotation, wouldn't we?"

"I'd rather sleep on broken glass."

"Oh don't be so virtuous, Jane. You may have my brother fooled, but I know what you really are."

It was a good thing the knives were out of reach. "Busy is what I am. And you're in the way."

"Stop all your chattering over there, Jane," Mrs. Allsopp said. "There's still plenty of work to do."

I tilted my head, giving Seth a challenging look. "Did you hear that? There's still plenty of work to do."

He nodded. "Yeah, I heard. Guess I best leave you to it."

* * *

The winter evening grew dark, the streets emptied, and the last of the customers vanished. I was up to my elbows in dingy dishwater and soap flakes.

Mrs. Allsopp cast another glance at the clock and shook her head. "Where in the world is Seth?"

Not only was Seth bumbling in later and later each morning, he'd started lagging in the evenings as well. And I'd noticed the money he brought in seemed slight compared to the amount of pies took out. Surely Mrs. Allsopp would catch on to this soon.

"Maybe he's stuck somewhere," Violet said as she twisted the drying towel inside one of the mugs.

Oh sure. Like a bordello or opium den.

Mrs. Allsopp wiggled into her pelisse. "Violet, dear, would you go check the Indian Head Tavern? I think he's spending some evenings there now."

"Yes, ma'am."

"And," she added, "tell him I said he's to bring home the day's taking before spending his share."

So she had noticed the shortage.

She wiggled her stumpy fingers into her gloves. "I'll see you girls in the morning." Then she was out the door.

Moments later Violet followed.

I relaxed, relishing the few minutes I had to myself. Leisurely, I went about wiping tables, lost in thoughts of Ichabod, wondering what he was doing at that moment—though likely scratching ink onto a document. My mind was solely with him when I happened to look up. A burly man in a black wool coat and beaver cap was staring at me through the window. Not staring...glaring. His face was shadowed by the lamplight of the street, but there was no mistaking his interest lay in something other than pies.

My heart skipped and I sucked in a breath. Quickly, I blew out the candle next to me, throwing my face into darkness. The man stood firm, his eyes boring into me. I felt like a snared rabbit, vulnerable and exposed. Why hadn't Mrs. Allsopp drawn the curtains?

Seconds later, he was at the door, rattling the knob rather than knocking. My instinct was to call out, "We're closed," but he couldn't have missed the sign in front of him saying as much.

Next he banged. I pressed myself to the wall, my heart in my throat. *Will he break in?* I could dally. I needed to arm myself. Which was easy enough with a kitchen full of knives.

I slinked to the kitchen passageway, but just as I was about to go through, someone came rushing out, nearly slamming into me. Jonas. He clutched my arms to steady me, then went to the door.

I slipped into the kitchen and peeked out, watching as Jonas opened the door a sliver.

"Can't you see we're closed?" he asked the man.

The man's voice rattled like a bucket of rusty nails. "I'm looking for a girl."

"Then I suggest you go down by the wharf," Jonas said. "You'll have your pick."

He attempted to shut the door, but the man bullied against it. "Not that kind of girl. I'm looking for a particular girl." He pulled a piece of parchment from his pocket, shook it open, and handed it over.

Jonas gave it a brief read, then handed it back. "There are no girls here by that name."

"What about the one I just saw through the window?" He peeked around Jonas, one probing eye finding a clear angle through the gap. "Does she work for you?"

Jonas's shoulders straightened as he stood taller to block the man's view. "You're referring to Jane Hanover. She's local. Grew up right here in Philadelphia."

"Are you sure about that?"

"Of course, I'm sure. And watch what you say. She and I are engaged to be married."

Oh, dear! A thousand thoughts wisped through my head. Why would he feel the need to lie? Had he thought of us

56

marrying before? Would I somehow be beholden to him now? But under these dire circumstances... *Bless you, Jonas.*

"Fine." The man stuffed the parchment back into his pocket. "Sorry to disturb you."

Jonas slammed and locked the door without another word.

I quickly busied myself, wiping down one of the chopping blocks I'd scrubbed a half hour before.

Jonas's footsteps were so light I felt him rather than heard him come in. He stood directly behind me.

"What did that man want?" I asked, failing miserably at keeping the tremble from my voice.

"It was nothing."

It was *not* nothing.

"Mistaken identity, I guess." His position shuffled. "He was looking for someone named..." He paused as though recalling. "Katarina."

He had to have heard my breath catch. I fought to steady myself. *Katarina.* He'd read my name in the dark doorway, seeing it briefly. I kept my back to him, continuing to wipe. "Why's he looking for her?"

He hesitated. I could feel his eyes on the back of my head. "Seems there's a nice reward for her capture."

I froze for a moment, stock still, then continued the chore. "Well, no wonder he was so eager. I'd probably be banging down doors too."

Silence. I still couldn't bring myself to turn and look him in the eye, which, of course, made me look even more guilty. "I want to thank you for defending me though."

"Ah, so you heard."

"A little."

"Well, he didn't look like someone to be trusted."

"Yes," I agreed, "it's hard to know who to trust anymore."

More silence, then: "Listen...Jane—"

I spun quickly. "If you came in search of your mother, she left about ten minutes ago."

His boyish expression gave him the appearance of a lost child. "No. Truthfully, Jane, I did not come to see Mother. I came to see you."

"Me? Whatever for?" A chill in my bosom alerted me that I was holding that stupid wet rag to my breast. I discreetly brought it down, still clinging tight to hide my lingering fear.

He waited, timid. Then said, "I know you're well aware of our financial situation."

Oh great. On top of it all, he's come to boot me out.

"And while I know little about your past, it's evident you have a keen knowledge of bookkeeping. So I came here hoping I could persuade you to have a look at our ledgers."

How could I concentrate on numbers now? Just because the burly man left didn't mean he'd bought Jonas's lie. He could be back tomorrow or the day after. I no longer felt safe here.

"Normally, I'd be happy to," I said, "but I'm feeling a little weary right now." An understatement to say the least.

His cheeks turned as pink as a baby's bottom. "Oh no, I didn't mean right now. They're not even here. I hoped that perhaps you would come to our home tomorrow night to look them over. Our hearth is much warmer and more comfortable than the one here. And I thought you might enjoy an evening away." Then quickly: "Not that I know your evening habits or anything, but…I just…"

Uh-oh. This proposal was an exceedingly bad idea. One that could eventually lead into an actual proposal. I didn't want to lead him on, have him think his lie to the burly man could become fact. "Thank you, Jonas, but I think maybe it'd be best if we worked here."

He stepped closer, pinning me against the chopping block, though his intentions didn't appear ill. "Jane, you work so hard. Just look at your hands." He took one in his, gingerly turning it back to palm, scrutinizing it like he would the inner workings of a clock. "I doubt this hand labored a day before you came here. Please, come to my home tomorrow night. You can sit back for a bit. Relax." He raised an eyebrow as a smile traced his lips. "There will be brandy and cakes."

Every part of me wanted to protest, but why? Secret plans were already formulating in my mind. I took my hand from him and forced a smile. "How can I say no to brandy and cakes?"

His face shot from glum to gleaming. "Wonderful. So I'll see you tomorrow evening? About eight?"

If I'm still in Philadelphia. "I toss the stragglers out early."

"Then tomorrow at eight," he said.

Yes. Now please go!

He stepped back, but dallied, like there was still something left unsaid.

To further encourage his departure, I went about removing my apron. As I strolled toward the stairs, I said, "Goodnight, Jonas."

I'd started up when he called, "Jane." I paused and looked back. His eyes had taken on a pleading nature. "*Is* your name Katarina?"

I looked him dead on. "No, Jonas. I promise you, it is not."

* * *

I shut myself in my room, heart pounding. Hurrying over to the bed, I pulled it away from the wall. Slipping my fingers into a rip in the mattress, I brought out a small newspaper clipping—one I'd folded and hidden inside.

Absconded from jail and wanted for murder and witchcraft by the magistrate and court of Sleepy Hollow, New York. Katrina Van Tassel. A girl of fair skin and brown hair. Eighteen years of age. About 5 feet 2 inches high. A reward of 300 pounds will be paid for her capture.

Three hundred pounds. To be paid by Magistrate Harding himself, I'm sure. With Father dead and our farm destroyed, he was now the richest man in Sleepy Hollow.

I'd to see to it he kept his three hundred pounds.

I stole a glance out the window at the alley below. The only stirring was a quivering dog digging through a trash bin. I bundled myself up for warmth and slipped out the back door. Then scurrying along the snow-shrouded streets, I made my way to the law firm where I knew Ichabod would still be copying documents and bothering over the cordwainers. Under normal circumstances, the brutal conditions would've rendered me numb. But tonight I burned with fear and anxiety, my heart keeping pace with my stride.

The law office was cramped between an insurance broker and a print shop with two small windows on each side of the door. I tried peering through one, but its heavy-woven curtains were too tightly drawn. But through the other, I could see a glimmer of candlelight. I pounded on the door with both hands. Moments later I heard the scratching of the latch being thrown, then Ichabod filled the doorway—his vest unbuttoned, his hair mussed, and his shirtsleeves rolled at the cuffs. Panic crossed his face. "Katrina." He quickly took my hand, leading me inside. "What's wrong?"

"*Everything.*" I fought tears, but they fell anyway. "I've been discovered."

He clicked the door shut, throwing the latch. "What?"

"A man came to the shop looking for me. He means to collect the reward."

"Did he see you?"

"Yes. But Jonas was there. He dealt with him." I thought it best to leave out his story of our betrothal.

Ichabod pulled a handkerchief from his pocket and dabbed my tears. "What does Jonas know of this?"

"Nothing. Though I'm sure he now suspects." A sob escaped me. "Ichabod, there would be no trial for me back there. I will hang."

He pulled me into his arms, his cheek to my forehead. "We must decide what to do."

"I've already decided. We leave. Now."

He squeezed me even tighter. "And go where? We have no horses. Little money."

I pulled away and looked into his eyes. "What about Connecticut? You could go home. Your friends will help us." Something that had been considered before coming here.

"No." He shook his head. "It's no different now. We'd still be putting them at risk."

I sagged against him, my thoughts tangled. My eyes darted about the polished office that contained two heavily carved rosewood desks, wingback chairs, and an elaborate shelving of leather-bound books. If anyone was truly at risk, it was Ichabod. This is the sort of office in which he belonged. Oh Lord, how much farther could I drag this man down?

I meant to sound emboldened, but my voice came out in a squeak. "Maybe I should go alone."

He tilted my face toward him, then pressing his palms to my cheeks—a bit too forcefully—he delved deep into my eyes. "Don't even *think* it."

"But, Ichabod, I'm holding you back. You've done nothing to deserve this punishment I've put upon you."

He lightly shook my head within his hands as though trying to rattle some sense into me. "I won't hear of it; do you understand? I ache for you enough as it is. The one thing that keeps me going is knowing that at week's end, I can be with you. I couldn't bear to be without you."

"But—"

"Promise me you won't go off without me."

"Ichabod…"

He shook my head again. "*Promise.*"

I nodded as best I could. "Fine. I won't willingly go without you. But if that man comes back…"

Ichabod drew me in, placing light kisses on my face. "Katrina, I won't let anyone hurt you, I swear. But we can't jump to rash decisions."

"Then what are we going to do?"

"For tonight, I'll escort you back and stay with you."

"But there'll be no place for you to sleep?"

"That won't be a problem." Taking my hand, he led me to a closet at the back of the office. Inside was pallet with a blanket and pillow. "I've grown accustom to making due."

"What? You've been sleeping here?"

"Not every night. But with the hours I'm keeping, it's become necessary."

This made me feel even worse.

He rolled his bedding into a tight bundle. "Let's go."

"But what about your work?"

His eyes cut to the corner desk. "Hammond can only expect so much of me."

He blew out the candle and we left.

When we got back to the shop, Violet was sitting on the kitchen stairs. "Jane, I was wonderin' where ya got off to."

Then she saw Ichabod, just behind me. She sat taller, her aqua eyes popping wide. "It's only Wednesday."

He raised a hand. "I know, I know." Then winking added, "I just have trouble staying away."

With a mixture of worry and wonder, she said, "Ya don't want me swappin' beds tonight, do ya?"

"No," I answered for him. "That won't be necessary."

She shrugged a shoulder. "Fine. I'm goin' up then."

"Violet," I said as she was pulling herself to her feet. "Did you find Seth?"

She rolled her eyes. "Indeed. Drinkin' away the pie money at the Indian Head. I brought the cart back. If I could, I'd knock 'im right in that pointy chin of his." She emphasized by making a fist.

A delightful image. "Only if I can get in the second punch."

She said goodnight and ascended the stairs.

Ichabod had gone into the dining area, closed off the curtains, and started a new fire in the hearth.

I peeked in. "I'll make some tea. Have you eaten?"

He paused to think. "Not for a while."

"I'll bring bread and soup too."

I hurried about the tasks, still trembling with trepidation. My icy hands didn't feel like my own. They disobeyed my commands to relax. Yet I managed the tea and food without disaster.

Once he'd finished eating, we laid down together next the fire. He wound his arms tightly around me, like swaddling a child. I needed that comfort more than ever.

"Ichabod," I whispered, "Will this madness ever end?"

He placed a tender kiss on my lips. "It will, Katrina. I promise you, it will."

I wanted to believe him, but honestly...how could he possibly know?

* * *

Ichabod snuck out before dawn, promising to check on me that night. I told him I'd be at the Allsopp's and should be safe there. Even if Jonas suspected me, I felt sure he'd never turn me in.

Every bone in my body creaked from sleeping on that hard knotty floor. But, then, I'd sleep on a bed of gravel if I could have Ichabod there alongside me.

I kept to the kitchen all day, letting Mrs. Allsopp work her magic with the customers. She had a way of filling their hearts as well as their guts, and even the bleakest of diners are known to spurt a belly laugh when she's serving. I stayed in the shadows, not trusting that the burly man had believed Jonas's story. If he had returned that day, I was not aware.

"I will see you very soon," she said to me that evening as she wrestled her round body into her pelisse and gloves. "I'll warm the brandy."

Once she'd gone, I handed Violet the broom. "It's your turn to clean the dining room. I scrub the pots and tins."

She batted her long copper lashes at me. "What? Ya don't want to sweep by the fireplace and recollect the tender moments hatched in yer little love nest?"

"Don't tease. I was feeling vulnerable last night and needed Ichabod nearby."

She took the broom and lightly tapped the handle to my forehead. "At least he was here to keep ya from sleepwalkin'." She then passed by me to the dining room.

"Make sure the curtains are drawn tight," I called after her.

* * *

Once the clean-up was done, I handed Violet her coat.

"But I weren't invited," she argued.

"I'm inviting you."

"Ya can't invite me to someone else's home?"

"I'll say that I was leery, walking the city at night. That I needed company." I seized her arm and began stuffing it into the sleeve.

"But what am I gonna to do while you're lookin' over their figures?"

"Eat cake," I said, stretching her coat around behind her to the other arm. I'd had easier times dressing my dolls as a child. "And besides, aren't you curious to see their house?"

She hunched her shoulders, fitting the coat into place. "Let me get my gloves."

I knew that would get her.

* * *

It was a few minutes after eight when Violet and I arrived at the Allsopp's home. It wasn't terribly far, but, I swear, the night was so brisk we had icicles hanging from our noses— even with my cowl hiding most of my face.

Jonas answered the door, a hint of surprise behind his eyes when he saw I wasn't alone.

"Jane made me come," Violet rattled out like a little girl tattling.

"It's quite all right," he said. *Was it?* "Please come inside."

Then his eyes caught mine. For a man struggling with debt, his smile was worth a barrel of gold. Maybe he thought I could turn things around for him, financially and *otherwise*. More than ever I was glad I'd brought Violet with me. Not only from any danger on the street, but also what I might encounter working so closely with him. I needed him to realize there could be no *us*.

Violet's eyes widened as she inhaled all that was quaint and comfortable about the Allsopp's home. I couldn't blame her. The tempting aroma of spices from the kitchen was enough to make me want to take a bite of the air. And did I smell a hint of orange marmalade?

"Yer home is wonderful," she said, removing her coat. "Like the ones on Nobbler Street back home."

I'll admit, if Nobbler Street had homes like this one, it's a place I might like to visit one day. Everything about this house spelled family—the china plates on the mantle, the samplers on the walls, and the piano-forte with its yellowed keys and worn pedals. But all the coziness soon fled when Seth came in from another room and dropped onto a large chair by the fireplace. "Ah, the girls are here." His tone was akin to someone who expected a package instead of company. A Seth-loathing chill wormed up my spine. Of course our loss was the Indian Head's gain.

"So Jane," he said, flashing his chipped tooth, "I can't wait to hear how you plan to fix all our financial woes."

I took the seat at the farthest end of sofa. "I'm afraid I can't fix them all. Your help might be needed with that."

He stretched, crossing his legs at the ankles and hands in his lap. "I've already given them my advice. They're none too keen to heed."

Jonas's sigh flickered a nearby candle. He smiled toward me from the tray where he was pouring the brandy. "Because we prefer common sense over half-cocked notions."

"The only thing half-cocked around here is you," Seth bit.

"I'm sorry if my rationality spoils your plans for ruination."

"Oh, shut your prissy mouth, you featherbrain. If you want to make money, you have to take some risks."

Violet and I shared a glance. Her eyes widened and she chewed her lip to suppress a laugh. I held back a chuckle too. These two were no different than the immature boys I grew up with in the Hollow.

"Right, Jane?" Seth said, catching me by surprise.

What? "I—uh—I..." He's asking me about taking risks? Ha!

I cast my gaze to Jonas, hoping he'd intervene, but he seemed as eager for my answer as Seth. And even more amazing, he wasn't showing the slightest bit of embarrassment from their childish display. "Well...I can't answer without knowing what those risks would be."

Seth sat forward, suddenly coming to life. He obviously cherished this so-called plan of his. "Here's my suggestion. We turn the shop into a proper tavern. One where folks would come for enjoyment, not to stuff their bellies. There'd be girls and plenty of entertainment, what with me juggling and Jonas playing the piano-forte." *So Jonas is the one who'd yellowed the keys.* "And trust me on this...I know for a fact that people are more willing to pay for rum than meat pies."

"Not decent people," Jonas tossed out. "And we've already discussed your part in helping out."

Seth scowled as he stretched back again and crossed his feet on the hob. "And I already said, breaking my back won't make up the difference in the loss from selling pies on the street."

Thankfully, it was then that Mrs. Allsopp wobbled in with a tray of cakes (and orange marmalade!). "Enough, you two!" She let out a whopping sigh and shook her head. "See what I constantly put up with?"

For the first time, Jonas blushed. The man could tinge more shades of pink than anyone I knew.

Violet hopped up and helped her with the tray. "This is mighty kind of ya, Mrs. Allsopp."

"Ah, it's nothing," she said. "We should've had you girls out sooner."

"She's right," Seth said, swaying his feet. "And often. It seems we barely know you." He cut his eyes to me. "And what secrets you might be keeping."

I started, nearly dropping the hot brandy Jonas was offering me. My flinching hadn't gone unnoticed by him. A look of disappointment washed over his face. Had he told Seth about the burly man? It didn't seem likely, but then again, I didn't expect to witness the sibling squabbles either.

I accepted one of the cakes, but the marmalade no longer held an appeal. *Just get this night over with and go.*

Another few minutes passed, all filled with small talk and awkward questions. Mostly to Violet about Ireland and which country she preferred. To their delight, she answered, "I prefer anywhere there's kind folks, a mattress, and enough food to keep me belly quiet." Her gaze wandered the room. "And maybe one day I'll live in a lovely house like yers."

Evil Seth choked on his brandy. I secretly hoped it'd strangle him.

Mrs. Allsopp reached out and stroked Violet's cheek with the back of her hand. "Thank you, dear. Mr. Allsopp bought this place thirty-seven years ago, when he was married to the first Mrs. Allsopp."

Now Violet coughed brandy.

"I've never mentioned it," Mrs. Allsopp continued, "but he was much older than me.

Almost twenty years." Her eyes sparkled. "He did have a young heart though."

A young heart that overextended itself. "And was he originally from Philadelphia?" I asked. I'd never questioned her about personal matters before now, worried it might open the gate to further questions about my own.

"Oh no, Mr. Allsopp was born in New Jersey." She turned, curious. "Have you ever been there?"

"Oh no," I answered, "I've never been anywhere."

Jonas laid tender eyes upon me. "And yet you speak like someone who has traveled the world."

I wish he wouldn't look at me like we were genuinely betrothed. "I assure you, I've only traveled by way of books and newspapers." The honest-to-God truth.

"And, believe me," Violet said, "Jane reads some fancy books."

Seth's eyebrows shot up. "Oh really? Where are you getting those fancy books, Jane? I don't recall the library being open on Sundays."

Panic crossed Violet's face and she quickly corrected her mistake. "I meant, she's not actually readin' 'em now. She *has* read 'em. She's told me some of the stories."

Jonas cocked his head, that look of infatuation still lingering. "Jane, I sincerely apologize. I hadn't stopped to think that you'd miss reading. Perhaps we can arrange some time together at the library."

"Yep," Seth said, slurping his brandy, "that'll make business flourish."

The only time I was thankful Seth existed.

I set my glass down on the coffee table. "This brandy is a bit numbing. Perhaps I should go over your accounts now while I'm still sharp."

Jonas hopped to his feet. "Of course." Placing a hand to the small of my back, he escorted me to the kitchen.

As we passed by Seth, he grinned up. "Go on then, Jane. Juggle us out of poverty." Jonas removed his hand long enough to slip a vulgar gesture at him, one he thought I couldn't see.

That's from both of us, I thought.

The kitchen felt more enclosed than the living room, its rafters low with hanging copper pots. And shelves filled with jars, crockery, and urns took up one entire wall. But what really drew my attention was the carving in the fireback, which took up most of the hearth. A man's face, surrounded by storm clouds, peered out through the flames, his expression poignant and sharp.

"Father," Jonas said. "He was an extremely vain man."

Ah, Mr. Allsopp, are those flames eternal where you are now?

I gave Jonas a slight smile. "Maybe he won't look so thunderous if I help his family."

"I never saw him look otherwise," he said, his voice cutting.

He led me to a small nook at the back of the kitchen, barely bigger than a closet. At one end was a small desk

74

topped with bills, receipts, and Mrs. Allsopp's ledger. Jonas retrieved an elbow chair from the kitchen and sat uncomfortably close to me. Thankfully there was no door to shut us away.

I set about rearranging the candles while Jonas opened the ledger to the latest entries. His proximity was like a stitch pressing into me, though I reminded myself it was better than that toothache known as Seth. Still, I think Jonas enjoyed the opportunity to be so near. Too near. He rested his wrist on the back of my chair as he leaned near my shoulder to observe.

The size of our work area contributed to the problem as well. I'd been used to my father's massive study, his large walnut desk, and the spacious walls that racked his muskets and pistols…and the prize sword he'd carried while serving in the Seven Years' War. There were times I got so sick of working the books that I wanted to run that sword right through me.

I went about bothering with Allsopp's figures, trying to keep my concentration there. Jonas seemed to be studying me rather than the tabulations. At times he hovered so close I could smell the sweet bouquet of brandy on his breath.

"Here's a problem," I said, pointing to an egg purchase recorded in the ledger. I laid the billing slip next to it. "It was entered incorrectly."

"That was not me," he spouted, a tad defensively. "That's Mother's handwriting."

"Yes,"—I nodded—"I know." I corrected it and moved on. A moment later: "Is this your handwriting?" I knew it was.

He leaned toward it and squinted. Not to judge if it was his writing, of course, but to see if he could spot the error before I named it. I gave him a moment for pride's sake.

"You neglected to carry over. See?" I corrected that one as well and smiled. "How about that? The Allsopps are now four pounds richer than when I first sat down."

He returned the smile even though his face had blushed the color of the brandy.

I went back to the numbers, running my finger down columns, flipping through receipts, and auditing to the best of my abilities. "Jonas, I don't want to tell you how to run your business, but it looks like you and your mother are quick to enter and add without checking each other's notations. Perhaps you could work out a system so that one of you does all the recording and the other verifies."

His eyes remained on the ledger as he ran his finger across his lip in thought. "Or perhaps we could work something out with you so that—"

"No." I laid down the quill and clasped my hands together, closing the rest of me off as well.

"Jane," he whispered. "You're invaluable. We could arrange for you to live here. Seth and I could share a room and—"

"No."

"But you said you'd better yourself if you could. So tell me. Why not?" His voice matched the pleading in his eyes.

I wanted to say something, but couldn't even conjure a good lie.

He rested his hand on mine and squeezed. "Please, tell me honestly. No more secrets. Are you from Virginia?"

What? I nearly choked on my surprise. "Virginia? Of course not. Why would you think that?"

His eyes ventured back and forth, searching mine for the truth. "I must know, *please.*" He no longer kept his voice low. "Is your real name Katarina?"

A crashing of glass startled us. We both whipped around to see Violet standing in the kitchen. She'd gone whiter than the snow dusting the windowpanes. Her brandy goblet laid shattered at her feet. "I'm so sorry!" Tears welled in her eyes. She quickly set about grabbing a rag to clean up the mess.

Jonas and I were on our feet as Seth and Mrs. Allsopp rushed in. Seth jutted his hip and crossed his arms. "And this is *exactly* why I won't teach you to juggle."

Jonas's face went tight with anger. He grabbed Seth's sleeve and twisted. "Would you please go away?" He winced when Seth grabbed his fingers and wrenched.

And I'd be bettering myself moving in with this?

Seth flung Jonas's hand from his arm and stormed out.

That's when I saw blood mixing with the brandy on the floor. "Violet, you're hurt." In her haste to clean, she'd run her hand across a shard of glass.

She slapped the rag to it. "I'm fine, Jane."

She wasn't fine.

"We'll bandage it," Mrs. Allsopp said, scurrying to gather more rags.

"I should go," Violet blurted through her tears. She shook like a stray dog in the rain.

"Calm down," I whispered, placing my arm around her as best I could.

"No, really, I should go." Her eyes were deep and despondent. "I'm feelin' tired."

Jonas took a clean rag from his mother and handed it to her. "Now that we're four pounds richer, I'll hire a carriage."

"No," she said. "I can walk."

"Then let me accompany you."

"No," she repeated, more defiant. "We'll be fine, won't we, Jane?"

As long as the burly man doesn't spot her. "Yes. We'll be fine."

After generous thank-yous all around, I led Violet out onto the brisk empty streets of Philadelphia, knowing that she was as much a criminal as I.

* * *

Violet sat on the bed, her eyes on her bandaged hand. It wasn't until I finished telling her of the burly man that she looked up. "Jane, what should I do?"

I admit, I was relieved that Sleepy Hollow had not found me, but my fear for Violet was just as great. "First I must know why he's looking for you."

She pulled her knees to her chest. "He's lookin' for Katereena, a runaway servant."

"From Virginia?" I didn't have to ask why she'd run away. The scars on her back were explanation enough.

"Yea. I came over two years ago as an indentured servant. I thought it'd be a dream come true. Regular meals. A real bed for once."

"What about your family in Ireland?"

"It was just pa and me till his drinkin' killed 'im. I was twelve. 'Cause I'm tall, I could lie about me age and get cleaning work and such. But even then I was livin' on the streets."

A pang of guilt shot through me, thinking of all those years of fine meals and rich desserts I'd indulged. Reality had yet to find me. "And your indenture?"

"Lots of people died on the boat comin' over. Ones that didn't starve were took by the sickness. I guess I'm sturdy stock. Or that's what the foreman from the Sidney Plantation said when the ship's captain auctioned us on the square. Turned out, Mr. Sidney, the man who owned the plantation, was a wretched old devil. Took his pleasure in people's pain. Mostly mine."

I traced a finger lightly along her shoulder. "This was his handiwork?"

"The beatin's were the easy part. He liked to torture me other ways too. Like makin' me stand naked with me arms over me head. He said if I lowered 'em even an inch he'd hack off me fingers."

"Dear God," I said, my hand over my mouth.

"Do you know what it feels like to hold yer arms up in the air for over an hour?"

"I don't want to know." I pushed the image of her suffering from my head. "You said you were naked. Did he ever...touch you?"

"I feared it at first, but he looked on me more with loathin' than lust."

"Did he treat all his servants that way?"

"Nay. But he talked to 'em like they was horseshit on his boots."

"Why do you think he singled you out for punishment?"

Here, she cocked her head in a "don't you know?" fashion. "Jane, he treated his slaves better than me, sayin' they was his own property and not filthy Irish."

Ah, of course. Anti-Irish sentiment was growing rapidly here. "How much would it cost to pay off your indenture?"

"He bought me for thirty-one pounds. I was to work it off in nine years. Though, if ya ask me, he earned every cent in the first month."

Thirty-one pounds was a lot to pay for "filthy Irish." But a stout, attractive girl like Violet would likely bring many bids.

She peeked under the bandage at the wound on her hand. "Do ya think Jonas knows it's me?"

"I honestly couldn't say. But he might suspect."

"The family needs money," she said, her eyes reflecting fear. "He might turn me to collect the reward."

Not Jonas. Seth, on the other hand. "I don't think he will. But perhaps we can talk to him, show him your scars."

She vigorously shook her head. "Nay, Jane. Let's not. We'll just keep it a secret until he asks."

"And what of the burly man? We'll have to keep you hidden in case he returns."

She curled into a tighter ball, new tears spilling. "Jane...do ya know what Mr. Sidney'll do to me if I'm dragged back there?"

I pulled myself closer and took her into my arms. "I won't let anyone take you. Ever."

"But how will ya stop 'im?"

I'd kill him if I had to. "I'll find a way."

She rested her head on my shoulder, her tears forming a wet ring on my dress. "Jane, I'm fearin' I've put you in danger now too."

I squeezed her a little tighter. "Believe me, Violet. I'm always in danger."

* * *

My heart dropped the next morning when I heard Jonas's voice. I paused on the staircase, casting Violet a nervous glance. She only stood taller and raised her chin. "Don't worry, Jane. I thought on it all night."

"Violet..."

She strutted down the stairs like royalty on rose-strewn carpet. I moused behind, unsure.

"Mornin'," she said, a tad too cheerful.

Mrs. Allsopp hurried over. "Oh, honey, how's your hand?" She was peeking under the bandage before the question was fully from her mouth.

"It's fine, Mrs. Allsopp. I was bein' stupid and careless. It's just that it startled me when I saw…" She took her hand from Mrs. Allsopp's and waved off whatever should've been trailing on the end of that sentence.

No, no, no, Violet. What story have you cooked up?

Jonas glanced toward me then back to her. "Saw what?"

She blushed a pink that clashed with her copper hair. Her eyes narrowed as her lips curved into a slight smile. "I think you know." She bounced around him, tightening her bandage back in place. We all gaped at her from behind as she tied on her apron and went about the morning like nothing was amiss.

"I don't know," Jonas finally said. "What'd you see?"

She twirled around, cut her eyes to me then him. Her eyebrow arched high.

Oh no, Violet, no!

Jonas waited a moment longer, looking two steps from strangling it out of her. Again: "Violet, what did you see that startled you?"

This time she tossed a glance toward Mrs. Allsopp and back in a *Do you want me to say it in front of her?* manner. My heart sank to my heels.

Jonas still hadn't a clue.

Violet cupped her hands around her lips. "I'm talkin' about when I saw you and Jane kissin'."

83

Jonas went a shade of pale that you only associate with graveyards and rising spirits.

I would've fainted dead to the floor, but that would've mucked up things even more. I planted my fists firmly at my hips. "Violet! You did not see us kissing!"

"I didn't?" She rose a little taller. "Hmm. Maybe I just thought I did." Then she winked at us. Winked!

Though Mrs. Allsopp had always treated me kindly, I learned right then I was made of in her eyes. Her scowl could've scrubbed the smoke stains from the ceiling. "Jonas?"

He held out his hands in a controlling gesture. "Mother, I assure you, she's mistaken."

"Indeed," I added.

"Jane and I were simply hunched over the books."

"And our backs were turned," I added.

"Oh!" Violet squeaked. She covered her mouth with her hand. "I'm so sorry. Now that I think about it, I never actually saw yer lips meet. And I guess with the shadows and the light and the..." She made back and forth motions with her bandaged hand. "I was mistaken." Her eyes rounded the three of us again. "But ya can imagine the surprise at what I *thought* I saw."

Phew! *Violet, you clever girl.* I couldn't be angry, even though her ruse came at my expense.

Mrs. Allsopp regained her composure. "Well...if it was just a silly mistake." She turned away and opened the butter crock, ready to resume a normal Friday.

Jonas stood a moment, looking conflicted. "Since that's cleared up and everything's fine, I'll take my leave." He turned, took two steps, then, without looking back, said, "And, Mother, had I actually kissed Jane, it would've been perfectly fine." The sharpness is his tone could've diced the carrots.

"Yes, son," she said, barely paying attention.

It wouldn't have been fine, but I understood he was just defending my honor. But there was still a lingering question in my mind. If Violet was now cleared of suspicion, would he again suspect me? I hurried behind him as he stepped out into the pale cold alley. "Jonas."

He turned, no smile.

I dawdled, then said, "I'm sorry about what just happened. You know how Violet is."

A shyness spread across his face and his nose scrunched. He took a moment to scratch it. "Yes, I know. She made a silly mistake."

"I-I just wanted to make sure you understood completely. My name is not Katereena. And I'm not from Virginia. I would swear it on a stack of Bibles."

New relief washed over him. "No swearing necessary, Jane. I believe you."

"Thank God," I said, relief filling me as well.

"It's nice to know my mother isn't harboring any escaped criminals."

I laughed a little too quickly. "No, I promise you, there are no runaways here."

His eyes narrowed as he considered me, blinking.

Oh rot! Never once had Jonas told me the burly man was after a runaway. Heat flooded my cheeks and it must've shown on my face.

"Have a nice day, Jane." He turned and strode away.

* * *

Regardless of what Jonas thought, the threat of the burly man still lingered. He obviously wasn't from the Sidney Planation or he would've known I was not Katereena. But Violet's auburn hair would likely be enough recognition for him. I made sure she stayed to the kitchen. When Mrs. Allsopp called for anything in the dining room, I volunteered. On Saturday, I assured Violet that when Ichabod (referring to him as Zachary) showed up, she and I could talk to him about the matter. That he could be trusted. Surely there was something in those law books that could help her. Thankfully, Ichabod was no longer worried on my behalf, having paid a delivery boy to inquire after me. Without detail, I'd assured him I was safe.

As every Saturday, the day dragged like a wet mop. I finished the last of the scrubbing and went upstairs. My heart double-thumped when I saw Violet buttoning herself into her usual Saturday night apparel. "What are you doing?"

She didn't look up. "What'da'ya think I'm doin'? I'm dressin' like Zachary."

"You can't go out. You'll risk exposure."

With her chin pressed to her neck, she continued the task. "But I'm dressed as a man. And I'm stayin' in a man's boardin' house. If that burly fella walked right by me, he'd be none the wiser."

"I won't hear of it," I said, swatting her uninjured hand away from the shirt buttons. "I couldn't live with myself if you came to harm on my account."

She returned a swat to my hand. "I decide things about me. Not you."

"No, Violet. I won't let you do this."

She looked one heartbeat away from slugging me. "I guess now that you and Zachary can cozy up on the floor, ya don't need me anymore?"

"You know it's not that."

"No one will recognize me, Jane. I'll stay locked in his room. And I'll only watch that gentleman across the hall through the keyhole. Same as always."

How could I get it through her head? "It's always been a risk. You know that."

"Then it won't matter."

"It *will*. It's more risky now than ever. So, no. *No*."

She snatched up *A Vindication of the Rights of Woman* and threw it against the wall. "The devil with ya!" She stormed out of the room and downstairs to the kitchen. Being half-dressed, she couldn't leave the shop. But that didn't stop her from kicking things around down there.

I sank onto the bed feeling like life had taken another great bite out of me. Ichabod would settle this. He'd know what was best.

* * *

Just after the stroke of nine, I heard him knock, then some mumbling between them. I was lying upon the bed, still in my ugly gray dress, not wanting to feel pretty or joyous. Upon entering, she pointed a stern finger in my direction. "Tell her," she said to Ichabod. I sat up, waiting for his response.

He said nothing at first, obviously not given time to think it over. His eyebrows rose as he gave me an inquisitive look.

"What has she told you?" I asked.

"That you've decided our weekly rendezvous now poses a greater risk."

I couldn't help but grin. "In those words?"

Adorably, he struggled against a smile of his own. Then more seriously, he asked, "What's happened?"

I patted the spot on the bed next to me. "Come have a seat."

After I gave him the necessary facts, embellished by several unnecessary details on Violet's part, he surprised me, saying, "I think Violet's right."

"Aha!" she crowed directly into my face. Then with a loud clap, pointed to Ichabod. "Zachary Crane, you're the smartest man I ever knowed."

I ignored her gloating. "How can you agree? She's taking a risk every time she sneaks into your room. This is double the danger."

"We'll take extra precautions", he assured me. "I'll see her safely to the carriage, continue on my way another street or two, then sneak back here." He turned to her. "And tomorrow I'll come for you. Do not venture out until I arrive. I'll figure a way to sneak you into the carriage and have the driver bring you straight here."

"Thank you!" she said, like a child given candy. "I promise to stay put in yer room."

I clutched Ichabod's sleeve. "You're willing to take this chance just to be alone with me?"

His expression said yes, but he added, "I really think it will be fine for tonight."

I was still fretful, but also thankful I wouldn't be losing my precious time with him. "You know I trust you." He gave me a slight nod. "But you..." I turned to Violet, doing my own finger pointing. "Swear to me there will be no peeking out."

"I swear."

"Not even at the tail-snapper."

"Not even at 'im," she vowed.

Ichabod's lips curved into a smile. He bundled her into his coat and together they snuck out.

* * *

"Well?" I asked when Ichabod returned.

"It's Philadelphia," he said. "No one thought twice about two young men hurrying along the streets, eager to get out of the cold."

I placed the back of my fingers alongside his pinkish nose. "We definitely need to get you warmed up."

Those were the last words spoken for some time.

After the lovemaking, which rid the chill like heated wine, we lay entangled, my cheek on his shoulder. Only then did my worries return.

"Ichabod," I whispered. "He whipped her with a lash."

His breathing slowed.

"He did unspeakable things to her." I turned my face up to search his eyes. "Surely there is some law against that."

He brushed some of my stray hair behind my ear. "I barely know Pennsylvania law, much less Virginia's. I'll see what I can do, but even the strictest laws can't touch the rich at times. He's likely a powerful man whose money feeds everyone within his share of the state."

I knew plenty about that, my own father's riches having once been the vein from which Sleepy Hollow flowed.

"Her only hope," he continued, "is for someone to buy off her debt. And even then there is no guarantee he would sell her."

I closed my eyes, facing a truth that had beaten me down since my escape. "It always comes down to money, doesn't it? Everything."

"Most everything."

Another reality opened to me—one that been a cruel itch growing with each struggle I faced. "Ichabod," I murmured, almost afraid to speak.

He must've sensed I was onto something dangerous because his breathing practically stopped.

Still, I went on, just as softly. "There is a fortune buried in Sleepy Hollow."

"No!" he snapped.

I shot up onto my elbow. "But we could devise a plan. Sneak in at night to retrieve it."

"No." His eyes glistened in the candlelight and there was no yielding there. "I will not watch you hang."

I worked to keep the pleading from my voice. "Perhaps you could go. It's not buried deep."

His lower lip trembled in anger. "And if I'm caught?"

Our gazes held as I realized the implication. They would do more than jail him. The magistrate would have him tortured in an effort to give up my whereabouts. Something Ichabod would likely take to the grave.

He sat up and bundled me in his arms. "Katrina. It is far too risky for either of us. Please, put it out of your mind."

While I agreed it was risky, I could never put it out of my mind.

* * *

My nights with Ichabod are usually dreamless. But tonight...

I'm back in the Hollow, slinking through the cemetery. I tighten my shawl as my breath hangs in soft mists before me. Though Marten's grave had no headstone, in my dream it does.

Marten Piers

1775 – 1793

He Took His Secret to the Grave

So many secrets, Marten. So many.

I kneel by the freshly-turned earth, my tears warm on my cheeks.
"*Marten, I'm so sorry.*"

*Though now my sorrow is no longer veiled in guilt. It was not I
who'd unleashed his executioner.*

"*You keep these,*" *I whispered, removing my glove. These being five
miniature clay roses from a bracelet he'd given me. How was I to know
each one contained a valuable blue diamond inside? I burrow a small
hole in the soil and, one by one, placed them inside.*

"*Goodbye, my sweet Marten. You will always be with me.*"

With me…with me…with me… He's with me. I suddenly
awoke to the *pull*—the one I'd become too familiar with of
late. He was out there. I anchored myself to Ichabod, who
snored softly beside me.

I will not come.

Why had the Horseman returned so soon? And did he
honestly expect me to leave Ichabod's side and ride away with
him?

Katrina.

No! I clutched Ichabod tighter. Had I not enough
worries? *Go haunt someone else.*

Katrina.

Damn him! I slipped out from under the covers and
threw on my nightdress.

Ichabod stirred, but did not awake.

I tiptoed to the window. The second my face was at the pane the Horseman drew his sword and aimed it toward me. An angry gesture. A command.

I will not come.

Katrina.

I stared down at him, the pull tugging me hard. *You want me? Come get me.*

Could he? Would he dismount?

Katrina!

The force of his demand gripped my heart and twisted. A pain, like a tightening winch, shot through me. I placed a fist to my chest, gasping for breath. I leaned against the seal for support. As he slowly turned the hilt of his sword, the pain grew to crippling measures. Black dots formed before my eyes. I had to go to him. Go or die.

Or...

"Ichabod!" I rasped.

In that instant the pain in my chest ceased. I stumbled back.

"Katrina?" In a snap, Ichabod was up at my side. "What is it?"

I took a moment to breathe. No need to look out the window. The pain was gone. The pull was gone. The Horseman too.

"I'm sorry," I said, moving into his arms. "It was just a bad dream."

The light from the window reflected the worry on his face. "Come." He led me back to bed. "Let me kiss it away."

Nightmares are never so easily erased.

* * *

Saturday was usually the one night of the week I felt safe and satisfied, waking on Sunday to the one person who made my life livable. Yet this one, filled with nightmares and ghosts, had me rising achy and tired. And much earlier than normal since Ichabod wanted to sneak Violet away from the boarding house before too many people were out and about.

"Maybe Violet and I should talk to Mrs. Allsopp," I said, helping him button up. Although unbuttoning him is more pleasing. "Tell her about the indenture."

"Can she be trusted?" he asked.

I lowered my gaze. I honestly didn't know what she or Jonas would do. They *were* harboring a criminal after all.

"And," he added, taking my hands in his, "if she knows Violet's past, might she pry deeper into yours?"

Oh dear. I hadn't thought of that.

He sat on the bed and drew me down into his arms, his shimmering green eyes apologetic. "Katrina, I wish there was something I could do to make things better."

I smiled, not wanting him to feel inadequate. "You can make things better by kissing me."

He did. Passionately. A kiss I wanted to stretch into forever. But, of course...

I walked him to the back door. "Be careful, my love."

"I will. And if there is *any* trouble this week," he said, "send word to me right away."

"That, or you'll find me on your doorstep again."

"I can't believe I'm saying this, but I hope that won't be the case. Not with bad news, anyway." He lingered, his eyes drinking me in. "I love you so much."

"I love you too." More than I could ever express.

We shared one more deep kiss, then he was gone.

I went back upstairs, busying myself with straightening the room. Not a minute later, I heard the latch on the back door turn.

Mrs. Allsopp, maybe? But she was an avid church-goer. And why would she come here on a Sunday? And so early?

I walked to the staircase. "Who's there?"

Silence. Then footsteps. Still, I saw no one. "Is someone down there?" No answer. My heart thumped. I thought of my final words to the Horseman last night. *You want me? Come get me.*

But a moment later, Seth appeared on the stairs, smiling up at me.

96

God, take me now. Yet there was some relief he wasn't a headless specter. "What are you doing here?"

He ignored my question and continued tramping up. I sensed he had a purpose. One I wasn't going to like. But then, I liked nothing about this man.

When he reached the top of the stairs, he cut his eyes away and brushed past me, into my room. The stink of whiskey trailed him.

I spun, my hands on my waist. "Seth? What do you want?"

He sauntered in a circle as though inspecting the place. "Well now, Jane…" I hated the glower on his face. "What do you think I want?"

Losing patience, I crossed my arms. "I'm guessing you're not here to teach me to juggle."

He grinned, his tongue peeking through that chipped tooth. "Nah. I'm here to get the same thing you gave that other fellow."

My face stung cold as my blood drained. "Other fellow? I don't know who you mean."

He strolled over, just an arm's length away. "Oh, yes, you do. You know exactly who I mean."

Think, Katrina, think! I pointed back toward the stairs. "Are you referring to the man who left a few minutes ago?" I tried a smile. "He was simply a diner who'd left his gloves here last night. He came back asking for them."

"Uh-huh." His eyes never left me. "And what about last weekend? What'd he leave here then?"

My heart volleyed in my chest. "Seth, you've been drinking. It's impaired your reasoning." The squeak in my voice betrayed me.

"No, no," he said, taking a step closer. "No impairment here…as you'll soon learn."

Get away from him now!

I turned to walk out, but he gripped my arm, squeezing. He pulled me close and placed his stinking mouth to my ear. "What do you think Ma's going to say when she finds out what her little pie-maker's been up to? Is he paying you to wrangle his eel?"

"You sicken me!" I tried to pull away but he gripped me tighter.

"And what about Jonas? He talks about you all the time, you know. If he finds out that his wonderful little Jane, with her perfect diction and lady-like airs, is nothing but a common whore, it'll break his heart into a million pieces." He touched his tongue to my ear. God, how I wanted to rip it out of that abominable mouth of his.

"I can explain," I whispered, tears springing to my eyes. Though, honestly, I couldn't. My mind raced for a clever lie.

"I don't want an explanation. I don't care. You can fornicate with that skunk every night if you want. I'm willing to keep your secret." His tongue trailed down my jaw. "For a price, of course." Bile rose to my throat as his hand strayed to my breast.

"Seth, don't do this, please. Just go." It was all I could do not to vomit all over him.

He made no effort to release me. "Now, Jane…you don't want me to go." He lightly kissed my neck. "Not without payment."

"Seth…"

"Cause if I do,"—another trailing kiss—"I'll go straight to my mother…" Another kiss. "And my brother…" And another. "And then you'll find yourself living out there in the alley."

"It would be my word against yours," I argued.

That brought a laugh. "True. Until I bring them here next Saturday night to show them what's going on. Or take them to that boarding house. I'm sure Violet would love explaining to them"—he squeezed my breast—"and all the men residing there, why she's putting on men's clothing and sleeping there."

Stars! He'd seen all. If he exposed us, Violet and I would both be put on the street.

"Seth, I beg you." *Oh, God, help me.* "Please. We can work out a different arrangement."

"Nah," he said, his stale whiskey breath making me gag, "I like this one." His hand fondled my breast as he sucked my neck and pressed the hardness in his breeches against me.

The sheer disgust prickled my flesh. But I would die before I'd let this happen. And there was still another option left. I whispered, "Seth, I know where there are riches."

He snickered, his mouth still on my throat.

"I'm serious. Let me retrieve them. I could pay off you and your family's debt."

"Ah...suddenly she's rich." I felt his chipped tooth rake my skin.

"You must trust me. It's there. And I would give it all to you. All." *Never.* "Then I'll go away. Be gone. For good. You'd never see me again."

He sucked in a breath, his brain drunk with sexual pleasure. "I don't want you gone, Jane. You belong here. Right here. Underneath me."

Not knowing what else to do, I spit in his face. That seemed to excite him more. The arm he'd used to grip me loosened, and he crossed it over my shoulder. Keeping me looped in his arms, he snaked his rough hand down to my other breast, working both of them the same way I kneaded pie dough.

I looked around. How soon before Violet returned? *Not soon enough.* "I have no other choice then," I whispered. "You win." I twisted around so my lips could meet his. It took everything in me not to spew in his mouth. Then, when I felt he was truly lost in the moment, the passion, I brought the heel of my shoe down hard on his toes.

He yowled an obscenity and loosened his grip. As he hopped back, I kicked him in the knee and ran. Though I saw nothing but free space before me, he moved quickly, catching me on the landing before I could flee down the stairs.

"Seth!" I gripped the railing with both hands. "Stop this! Please! It's insanity."

He grumbled under his breath as he put his arms about my waist and pulled. I held on with a raw strength that only accompanies panic. Unless he planned to pry each of my fingers loose, it was fruitless for him to continue his yanking me.

"Fine then." He stopped his tugging. "We'll take care of business right here." He bunched my skirt and petticoat and lifted, intending to take me in animal-fashion.

"No!" I swung around and glommed onto his collar, intending to shove him down the stairs. But my rage and momentum—and that raw strength—increased my physical mobility. Rather than pushing him forward, I thrust him over the side. He fell, his head striking the edge of a butcher block just before hitting the ground. He laid sprawled on his stomach, his cheek pressed to the floor, one arm twisted in a manner that suggested it was broken.

I stared for a moment, my chest heaving. *Oh dear God.* "Seth?"

Nothing.

I cautiously took the steps. "Seth?" Still no answer. Then I saw blood pooling around his flattened cheek. "Seth? Seth?" I knelt over him. His breathing was shallow, but thankfully there.

He was alive, but my position with the Allsopp's? Probably deader than the Horseman himself.

I could think of only one way out of this tangled mess. I leaned close to his ear. "Seth, can you hear me?"

His fish mouth worked as if he wanted to speak. Then in a low grumble, he uttered, "You mangy flea-bitten pus-sucking whore."

I sighed in relief. "Oh good. You can hear me."

He groaned.

"Listen to me. I did not lie about the riches. I know where they are. I'm going now to retrieve them."

His eyes cut upward, catching mine. "You broke my arm, you bitch."

"Truthfully, I think your head is broken more." Though that juggling arm was far more valuable to the Allsopp's.

I went for a rag and wetted it, then gently lifted his head, discovering a gash just above his brow. I pressed the rag to it and laid his head back down.

I rose and looked about the kitchen. This was no time to tarry. I rushed to pantry, snapped open a linen bag and hurriedly filled it with sustenance for my journey—apples, carrots, some dried pork. *How much will I need?* I tried calculating the days, trying to remember how long it had taken Ichabod and me to travel the distance. Those were hazy memories though, time spent in trepidation and shock.

"Jane…" Seth's eyes were batting, fighting to stay open, but on me nonetheless.

No time for him now. Using the back of an old tally sheet, I wrote Violet a simple note, praying that her reading skills had advanced enough to make it out.

Went for money. Do not tell Z. until you must. Will return within a fortnight. Stay safe.

I pinned the note to Seth's breeches so she'd see it right away.

"Doctor…" he mumbled.

"Violet will be here soon. She'll fetch a doctor. I promise you won't die before then."

When I rose he reached for my ankle, then yelped in pain.

Snatching up my cloak and gloves, along with the bag, I rushed to the door. *Wait!* I remembered. I'd need a weapon. Veering back around the ailing puddle that was Seth, I grabbed a butcher knife, rolled it in a towel, and placed it in the bag too.

Back at the door, I said, "I *will* return with riches, Seth. To pay off your family's debt." *And Violet's.* "Keep that in mind as you conjure whatever ridiculous story you plan to tell them. And if you don't paint an ugly picture of me, I may share a little extra with you."

Then I fled.

*** * ***

Don't think, don't think, don't think, I repeated as I hurried along the backstreets of Philadelphia. I willed the morning sun to appear, but no such luck. It continually lost its battle with a blanket of snow clouds, leaving me feeling hemmed under a gray dome. Church bells tolled, horses clomped, and my heart kept rhythm with my pace. I only slowed when I neared the estate outside the city—the one where Dewdrop was stabled.

Don't think, don't think, don't think. I hid behind a sugar maple, peering around. No sign of the ill-tempered man or his hairy mole. But he could be inside. And Dewdrop? What if the owner had ridden her to church? *Don't think, don't think, don't think.*

I managed to climb the fence undetected. Since the stables had no windows to peek in, I took my chances slipping through one of the red arched doors. Ah! The smell of hay. Something I hadn't encountered since leaving home. I inhaled, filling my lungs.

Though the sun was absent that day, my stars had aligned. Dewdrop was there, third stall. She perked when seeing me, snorted and bobbed.

I placed a finger to my lips. "Shh…" Finding a suitable saddle and bridle, I quickly went to work. One more crime to add to my growing list of sins. *You're not stealing her, only borrowing.*

As I hurriedly led her out, I nearly stepped into a massive pile of horse manure. Which of course reminded me… *Seth.* I hoped Violet had found him by now. *Don't think. Don't think. Don't think.*

I didn't think. I acted. And moments later I was racing away. Back to Sleepy Hollow.

Part Two

Return to Sleepy Hollow

I didn't slow until I felt it safe. But would it ever be? I was now a vulnerable traveler, alone on the road—the bitter cold eating away at me.

I worked to keep my mind on my destination and the diamonds, not on how long I'd be journeying to get there— *four days? five?*—or how I might slip in, uncover the jewels, and be gone without anyone spotting me.

Other woes weighed on me too. How deep had I buried the diamonds? Had heavy rainfall washed them away? Could someone else have found them? And least important, but still a curious question...where had Marten gotten them? Which port had he smuggled them from? I had read reports of the crown jewels of Louis XVI being stolen over a year ago, including a particularly large diamond known as "French Blue." Had I buried cut portions of it?

I'm not sure how many miles I braved that first day. Or the next. Anytime I came to an unfrozen brook or stream, I stopped so Dewdrop could drink and rest. She nibbled on the brown stubble that sprouted up through the snow. I ate sparingly.

On two of the evenings we found refuge in someone's barn. There, Dewdrop ate her fill of hay. I'd manage five or six hours of restless sleep, then we were out again, facing the brutal temperatures. Determination drove me...as well as thoughts of Ichabod. This would all be over soon. We could afford to marry. *And I'd never have to endure this ungodly cold again.*

I avoided the towns as much as possible. Anytime I met a passing traveler, I kept my cowl low. I was not blind to my vulnerable situation. A young woman riding alone. *A wanted woman.*

Once I reached the Hudson, I remained close to its shores. I'd once told Ichabod, "As long as you can hear the river, you'll find your way back." For me, at that time, there was no more joyous sound.

But the lack of sleep and raw air made me their victim. I'd nodded off a few times, catching myself as I began to slip from the saddle. My body had given way to hunger too. Finally, late afternoon of the fourth day, I reached familiar territory. My heart sped. *Familiar territory?* Enemy territory. Should even one person spot me, by that time tomorrow I'd be swinging from a noose. But I stayed off the main roads, avoiding the heart of the village. I skirted to a cliff above the river. There, I hid in the safest place I knew. An old abandoned granary at the back of my father's farm. My sacred spot. A place that I'd called *Bliss.*

The door sang its usual creak as Dewdrop and I took shelter inside. I trudged up the stairs to the top where I'd played often as a child. So many plans had been made there— before and after I met Ichabod. My tea set and paper dolls were all still there. As was the old patchwork quilt. I peeked out the small crusted window to the snow-laden meadow below. A sight I'd seen so many winters before. Then, kicking off my shoes, I curled into the quilt and slept like the dead.

Dewdrop's snorting awakened me, but I didn't immediately sit straight up. Instead, I stared into the darkness, wondering about Philadelphia and the people I'd left behind. Seth's arm would be set by now, but what about Violet? Could the burly man have taken her this week? And Ichabod? Had Violet told him I'd left? I heaved a weary breath. *Come on, Katrina. Nothing gets resolved by lying around contemplating..*

I sat up and felt for my shoes. *What time is it?* I opened the window hoping to judge by the night sky. Some clouds had thinned, stars winking though. *Ten o'clock? Eleven?* I reached into my bag and pulled out an apple. *Hmmm...* Even if the townspeople weren't tucked in and sleeping, they'd be inside by their warm hearths. Well...all but the drunks at the River Song tavern. They'd be easy to avoid though. Especially if I took the shortened path and rode through the fields of our farm.

I was told after Father was killed the place had been ravished and plundered—the townspeople taking away everything they could carry. God knows what else they'd done to our home. I wouldn't be surprised to find it burnt to the ground. Not something I was anxious to confirm, but I couldn't help but wonder. *And it is the quickest route.*

After a few more bites of the apple, I gave the rest to Dewdrop and patted her muzzle. "We're halfway done, girl." And though I knew no one was about, I peeked out the granary door before opening it wider. Then leading Dewdrop out, I mounted and rode off without a single glance back.

Resting at Bliss had worked like a tonic for Dewdrop, adding extra friskiness to her step. Or maybe it was just the feel of home that had enlivened her.

As we reached our fields, I reigned her to a slower pace, gaping at what I saw.

What in the blazes?

I'd expected them to be empty, overgrown, and buried beneath the snow. Yet they thrived with winter crops and fattened livestock. *Who's farming the land?* Maybe cutting through was a risky choice after all. Still, I had to know.

I rode up behind the row of slave shacks. I saw no candlelight inside, though smoke rose from the chimneys. *Should I knock? Wake them for answers?* No. My presence there would only endanger them.

But curiosity ate at me. I rode quietly, in shadow, until I reached the stables. *Freshly painted? What is this?* I reigned Dewdrop behind it to keep her out of sight.

Staying to the trees, I crept toward the house. Though darkened and closed, it looked exactly as it had four months ago when I'd been arrested and jailed. Riches, not ruins. But who'd taken over our property?

Slinking to the front, I saw the honeyed glow of candlelight coming from one of the parlor windows. I crossed to the side and pressed my back to the wall, beneath the darkness of the eaves. Spying would be easy enough, but it meant removing my shoes so there'd be no clunking echo on the floor of the piazza. First one. I stepped up. *Lord, that's cold!* Then, catching my breath, the other. I sneaked around, my back against the wall. With luck on my side, the tapestry curtains were parted a bit, allowing me to peek in.

Son of a... The magistrate sat napping in Father's overstuffed chair. *The magistrate!* I should've known. My blood rose, bringing warmth to my numb ears. Other parts of me thawed too. All but my heart. *How dare he lay claim to our property?* The second richest man in Sleepy Hollow was now the richest—profiting off our misfortune.

I turned back to the wall, seething. I took a moment to indulge myself, conjuring a fantasy of bursting in and beating him with that staff he sometimes carried around.

Oh, why should I even care? I came for the diamonds. *Just unearth them and go.* This time next week things would be different. I dared one last glance. The magistrate slept on, his

111

round belly swelling and ebbing with each mellow breath. *You wretch.* It was at that moment that the mantel clock chimed, causing him to start. Me too. I pulled away quickly, flattening myself to the wall. The clock continued, striking eleven times. At least now I knew what time it was.

Ever so quietly, I tiptoed off the piazza, put on my shoes, and hurried to the stables. Then Dewdrop and I were off, sailing away from the farm and on to the graveyard.

* * *

The Sleepy Hollow cemetery lies adjoined to the church, though I doubt in a time of need I could find sanctuary there. I'm sure the reverend would like to see me hang as much as anyone. Thankfully, he was also a fat old crank who took to bed early. No worries of seeing him there.

I hitched Dewdrop under the bridge and then swept through the cemetery till I came upon Marten's grave. The tombstone in my dream had only been fantasy, of course. But one had been erected. Small, simple.

Marten Piers

Born 1775

Died 1793

Beloved Fisherman

Since Marten was an orphan, I suspected his marker had been paid for by Notary de Graff, the father of Marten's best friend. I hold only fond memories of the notary. He was more than kind to me. And looking upon this gravestone...well, I loved him even more for this.

My heart thumped like a land-bound fish as I knelt at the spot where I'd buried the jewels. I brushed away the frost. *Please be here. Please. Please.* Removing my right glove, I proceeded to burrow into the frozen ground. Not so easy. In my haste to get here, I'd forgotten one essential thing—a tool for digging. Even a small spoon would've done the trick. *Please be here.*

With no light to see by, I searched in darkness. Digging and sifting. *Please be here.*

But what if they're not? What will await me back in Philadelphia? *Please.*

My silent prayer did not go unanswered. Within a minute I unearthed them. Even mucked in dirt they still held a gleam. I carefully tied them into my handkerchief and tucked it into my bodice, snug between the crevice of my breast. *Thank God!* At that moment, I was inflated with a joy so tremendous, I felt I could fly back to Ichabod.

It was then that I heard it—the thunderous sound of hooves pounding earth. I whipped around too late. With lightning speed, the Headless Horseman was on me.

"No!" I screamed as he clasped a handful of my cloak, lifting me like a puppet. I flailed, trying to untie the drawstring—to fling my cloak away and free myself. But he was too quick, pulling me close and wrapping his arm around my waist, my feet kicking air.

"No! No! Please! I cannot go with you."

While I fought and clawed, he drew his sword. *Merciful Heavens!* I was about to lose my head! But instead of slicing through my neck, he brought the hilt down hard, striking it to my temple. I felt the force of it near my eye. A myriad of sparkles burst before me...then nothing but pure black.

* * *

I awoke, veiled in darkness. Full darkness. The kind that mashes against your eyes and you try to blink away. I put my fingers to my face, crawling them over my cheeks, eyelids, and brows. *Heaven help me, am I blind?* And, oh, my head throbbed. *The Horseman! Is he still here?* I lay stiff and supine, the perfect specimen of stillness just in case. Well, not perfect. My ragged gasps had me heaving like there was little air to be found. Which felt true. I breathed in dust and the foul odor of decay. It took restraint not to cough it up. But instinct told me he was not present. *The diamonds?* I reached into my bodice. He had not taken them.

"Anyone?" I said, to test my voice. It echoed in the void.

I slowly drew my knees upward, aware that I was lying on a wooden floor. *But where?* One thing I knew for sure, this was not the afterlife. Or was it? Hell is a black pit after all. I reached my hand up, wavering it above me. *Blazes!* Every motion was an agonizing reminder I'd been conked on the head. I touched the lump where he'd struck me. Tender, but no blood, fresh or dried. Blinded or not, I had to get away.

With the quickness of a crippled snail, I sat up. With that effort behind me, I only needed to rise. *Carefully...* One step later, I fell, crashing down, elbows banging on the ground. My head and arms screamed with pain. As did I as well. What had I been lying on? Some type of bench? Using it for support, I dragged myself upward and turned. Then I saw it—a teeny ribbon of light within the dark. *Thank God, I'm not blind!*

Light. *Light!* It had to be a way out.

I crawled toward it, carefully running my hands over the ground in front of me in case any more surprises were in store. Once I reached the rim of light, I touched the surface from which it came. Wood. I slid a palm over it. A door! I felt my way up until I found a handle and...

Had I really thought it'd be unlocked? I rattled it over and over. *Open, open, open!* The most it did was allow in a bit more light. Daylight. Whatever or wherever this room was, it led directly outside.

I pounded hard, head throbbing with each thump. "Help! Help!" But just as quickly, I slapped my hand over my mouth. *Think, Katrina.* I was likely still in Sleepy Hollow. Any rescue I'd receive here would be short lived. The townsfolk would simply deliver me from this prison to another. I stood a better chance with the Horseman. My only option was to escape without aid.

So the door was useless. Unless I found a key. *Not likely.* No windows. *What is this place?* Again I crawled on hands and knees, keeping to the walls and working my way around its diameter, one corner at a time. It couldn't be a root cellar, there were no stairs or incline of any sort. A springhouse of some sort? No. Who'd want to store food in such a foul-smelling hole?

But the room was small. Even smaller than the one I shared with Violet. I then crept toward the center, where I sensed the bench would be. I rose to my knees, running my hands over it. Not a bench, a box. As I worked my way around it, my foot tapped against another solid object, practically identical. I gasped with realization. *Oh, Katrina, no!* I was locked inside a crypt.

I stumbled back to the door and reached up, feeling for what I knew would be above it. As I feared, it was there—a winged angel carved into the stone. This was not just any crypt. It was in the Van Tassel crypt. I'd been locked inside with my parents' rotting corpses.

* * *

I foolishly rattled the door like determination alone would magically open it. Though I was blinded by darkness, one thing was crystal-clear. If I didn't get out, I'd wither and die. *God forbid, the smell alone might kill.* Ichabod would live out his life in wonder, never knowing where I'd disappeared. Maybe I'd be better off taking my chances with the magistrate after all.

I pummeled my fists against the door, ignoring the pain in my head. "Help! Help! Someone!" But the Van Tassel crypt was in the outer part of the cemetery, far from the church. Who would be around to hear my cries?

My stomach cramped from hunger, and my throat was as dry as a sun-beaten rock. All that screaming had made it raw and sore. I wilted against the frigid stone wall and sank to the floor, my cloak bunching behind me as I slipped down. Laying my forehead upon my knees, I forced back tears. After all, crying would only add to my parched condition.

All those nights I'd wondered about the Horseman. Where he'd take me. Was this his plan all along? To seal me in with my dead parents? It made no sense.

I rubbed the spot where he'd struck me, wondering how long I'd been unconscious. All night, obviously, but what time was it now? The teeny light stream being winter-gray, made it difficult to judge. But I'd have bet it was afternoon.

Since self-pity wasn't helping my cause, I inched my way around the perimeter of the room, hoping to find *anything* to aid my escape. But the crypt was built into a small hill, and the only way out was through the door. Feeling defeated again, I leaned against Mother's coffin, conjuring an image of her in life…before growing ill. So filled with beauty. So full of life.

Mother, if ever I needed to see a ghost, it's now. Please come to me. Tell me what to do.

I waited for a sign. Nothing. Had I honestly expected an answer?

I couldn't bring myself to ask Father, of course. I was the reason he lay here cold.

I wrapped my cloak tighter around me—*I will not cry. I will not cry*—and climbed back onto Mother's coffin. I curled into a ball and rested my weary head on my arm. Closing my eyes, I thought, *I cannot die here.*

* * *

The magistrate parades in, holding up the warrant for my arrest. He pushes it close to my face. "Katrina Van Tassel, you are under arrest for the murders of Garritt de Graff and Marten Piers."

I clutch the sofa for support, my heart thundering, my face flush.

Father strides forward and rips the warrant from the magistrate's hand. "You have the audacity to come here with these ravings of madness!"

Harding turns on Father. "Baltus, she is a witch!"

"How dare you?" Father strikes the magistrate with the back of his hand.

"On what grounds are you accusing me?" I challenge, trying to hide my fear.

A vicious smile spreads across the magistrate's face. "Oh, Katrina, you tend to leave an untidy trail."

The image of that nasty smile caused me to jerk awake. The blackness shrouding me hung even darker. Wait. It wasn't the dream that roused me. There was rustling outside. How I wished at that moment that I were a witch so I could conjure a way out of this ghastly prison!

A rattling, only slightly louder than my drumming heart, sounded at the door. Then it opened. The winter clouds had parted, allowing a moonlit glow to shine upon him. *The Horseman.* I'd never seen him off his mount. He tossed back his cape, revealing rows of brass buttons and military galloons on his coat.

With fear driving me, I fell off of Mother's coffin and scooted to the corner, drawing myself into a tight ball. *God, help me!*

He closed the door, sealing us both into darkness. I waited, every inch of my body lit with dread.

There was scuffling by Father's coffin, then a flare of candlelight upon it. First one, then two. I heard no striking from a tinderbox, so I assumed he lit them using supernatural means. I blinked against the brightness, my eyes adjusting. *Whatever he has planned for me I'd rather not see.*

The Horseman tarried a moment then strode toward me, holding a bulging bag. My blood drained. *Was he collecting severed heads?*

Heart pummeling, I crouched even lower, shielding my own with my arms. "*Please,*" I croaked in a whisper.

He towered a moment, but instead of separating my head from my body, he tossed the bag toward me. It hit one of my sore elbows and dropped to the floor, thudding like a sack full of melons. He then retreated back to the door and leaned against it, arms crossed.

I still dared not move, not an inch. Though I could not quell the tremors that overtook me.

If not my head, what does he want?

We both remained in our positions for a full minute or more. Then, as though sighing impatience, he stomped toward me, withdrawing his sword.

"Please," I repeated. I couldn't hunch any lower.

But instead of running me through, he sliced the cloth sack, spilling its contents. Yams, squash, crabapples, chestnuts, and dates. All stolen from someone's cellar, I assumed. Among the food was something I treasured more. A water flask.

He again withdrew to the door. With quaking hands, I uncorked the flask and gulped half its content. The cool water eased my throat, but did nothing for my nerves. I stayed huddled in the corner, holding the flask to my breast as though he might rip it away from me.

Again, we waited. Me, recoiled and cautious. Him, leisurely guarding the door, the tip of his sword touching the floor. Finally, I asked, "What do you want with me?"

He made no effort to answer. But could he speak? One usually needs a head to converse. Yes, I'd heard him call my name, but that came more as a feeling than a sound.

"Please," I begged him, "let me go."

No movement on his part. And the only sound was a small crackle from one of the candles propped on Father's coffin.

The seconds beat away as I waited for some indication from him. After a few moments he angrily kicked the heel of his boot to the door and came over again. Using his sword, he speared a squash and held it in front of me. *If he wanted to kill me he wouldn't feed me. Would he?*

Rather than risk touching his blade, I picked up another squash from the spilled bag. My stomach cramped from hunger, but I was too frightened to eat. *If only I knew his purpose.* Why would he want me here...alive? Was he doing someone else's bidding?

He flicked his wrist, popping the vegetable off his sword. It fell next to my feet. This time, rather than the door, the Horseman trod to Father's coffin and sat on the end opposite the two candles.

My eyes cut to the door and back. It bolted from the outside. *Did he leave it unlocked?* Was there some way I could overpower this ghost and flee? The butcher knife that I cleverly brought with me was still towel-wrapped in the bag strapped to Dewdrop's saddle. Then a new thought hit me. Dewdrop! *Oh my!* The entire village knew my horse. If someone had found her—which they most probably had— the magistrate could have men looking for me right now. I didn't know whether to cringe or rejoice.

The Horseman sat rigid, as though expecting something from me. Then I realized what it was. I took a bite of the squash. Though still ripe, its firmness had given way, making it soft, like biting into a pear. But I didn't care. I was so hungry I could eat sawdust.

Once I'd begun to eat, the Horseman relaxed, tapping his sword to the toe of his boot.

I kept my eyes on him, the coffins, the candles…anywhere but the door. Yes, there could be further danger awaiting me outside, but it was a chance I was more than willing to take.

After I'd eaten the squash, I took another long swallow from the flask. "Thank you," I said sweetly as I set about gathering the scattered harvest he'd brought. One of the crabapples had rolled close to Mother's coffin, halfway between me and the door. I kept my gaze on it as I crawled over, reaching out. *Easy. Easy.* Then, in one swift effort, I shot to my feet and dashed.

With the speed of a deer, the Horseman leapt over Mother's coffin and placed the tip of his sword to my jaw. Anger rose, circling him like an aura. With his sword firmly pressed to my neck, he backed me across the room to the far wall.

I lowered my eyes to the gleaming blade and my own anger followed. "You shouldn't even be here," I whispered. "I sent you away."

His hand trembled as though resisting the urge to run me through. Then he spun away and stormed out the door.

There was no need to test the handle. I knew it was locked. Though still surrounded in peril, I sighed relief. At least he'd left me with food and light, and my shadow to keep me company.

* * *

Conserve and survive. I quickly blew out one of the candles, throwing the crypt into half-light. This was a "just in case" measure. I'd planned to be out of there before the first candle guttered to a near demise.

The pain in my head had now subsided, and with my thirst quenched, my mind ran clearer. I looked around the crypt, now pooled in a dim yellow glow. *Think, Katrina, think.* I needed to get out *now*, under the veil of night. I could then make my way to the river, hide till morning, then stow away on an unsuspecting cargo boat. If it took me only as far as the city, so be it. I would find my way back to Philadelphia from there.

I picked up the lit candle and searched the wall that surrounded the door, carefully running my finger over the mortar. Surely there'd be some crack or crumble to serve as a starting point for my escape. *Criminy!* Barely a dimple. The mason who'd crafted this mausoleum must've thought he was entombing royalty. I then studied the door hinges. There were three, all long strap hinges with curved pins that would easily lift—if the door was open and I had the strength of a gorilla! *Sigh.* My only option was to dissemble the hinges. This could only be done by removing the rusty nails. And since it would be impossible for me to extract the ones attached to the stone wall, I'd have to take out the ones on the door itself. All fifteen of them!

I tested each, seeing which ones I could easily slip a fingernail behind. Only two, but that was a start. Now I just needed a tool—something that would allow me to extract the nails.

I went back to the corner and plopped myself down, my back resting against the wall. *Think, Katrina, think, think, think.* Being in dire need of nourishment, I snatched up a yam and bit in. *Think, think, think.* What could I use to pry a nail? I had absolutely nothing on me other than the Diamonds. No keys or tweezers or button hook. Nothing.

Wait...

I had nothing, yet someone here did. The air thinned, and the yam soured in my mouth. I cast my eyes to Mother's coffin. *Oh, Katrina.* My hands trembled and I fought to steady my breath. Her necklace, a brass heart-shaped pendant, about an inch in diameter, open in the center. It was a treasured keepsake she wore always, even in death. I set the yam aside and took a healthy swig from the flask. *God, there's got to be another way.* I waited for divine intervention. None came. To escape, I had no other choice but this.

I rose on wobbly knees and skulked over to her coffin. *This is what she would want,* I told myself. Yes. She'd encourage me to rob her corpse if that's what it took.

I averted my eyes, sucked in a breath, then pushed against the lid. It was heavier than I expected, but I managed to scoot it, unleashing a stronger scent of rot. My stomach rebelled, but I vowed, *I will* not *vomit that bit of yam all over Mother*. With my gaze still on the wall, I quickly removed my cloak and draped it over her bones, not wanting to glimpse her this way. I called up the memory of her face moments after she'd died. Sallow and pale, a pleasant smile curving her ashy lips. Only being twelve at the time, I told myself she was smiling at the angel who'd come to escort her to the heavenly gates. Though now I wondered if her smile was simply a show of relief for being spared further pain. What I did *not* want was the imprint of her withered skull forever seared into my mind.

I placed the candle on the skewed lid, then, gingerly pulled my cloak aside just enough to reveal her neck, now a brown knotty stump of bone. But I had exposed the clasp of the necklace. That was enough.

This was not my first time to rob a grave. Just months before I'd dug in the cemetery to remove the skeleton of a murdering ghost. I flung his filthy remains into the freezing waters of the Hudson, thinking the current would carry his apparition with it. *I sent you away.* Had it worked, I wouldn't be in this situation now.

I'd hoped removing the necklace would be quick work, but a piece of the chain had settled within the column of her neck bone. I worked and wiggled, trying to distance the fact that this was the woman who'd rocked me to sleep at night. *This is what she'd want.* Finally it plucked loose.

Once I'd removed it, I set the candle on the floor, removed my cloak (eyes averted) and pulled closed the coffin lid. And though I was led by desperation, I couldn't help wonder if I'd wear this moment like a scar. *Only if I get out.* I hopped to my feet and got busy.

Finding the loosest nail, I wedged the pointed end of the heart behind it and yanked. It did little more than send tiny grains of red rust to the floor. I then hooked the pendant behind it and pulled outward. It budged a hair. *Blast!* It's not like I hadn't uprooted nails before. I thought it would be easier than this.

I sucked in a breath and pulled again. For my effort, I'd managed another fraction of an inch. I had no idea the length of that stubborn nail, but one thing was clear, removing it would take *much* longer than I'd anticipated. And if successful, hurrah, I only had fourteen more to go. But what other choice did I have?

I'm not sure how long I struggled with the nail. It seemed at least an hour. Then, finally, out it popped! "Aha!" I gazed on that rusted three-inch spike like it was a magic key. Now I had another tool at my disposal.

I ran it through the top of the heart, turning the nail into a lever. I then found the next loosest nail and got to work. My tool lost value quickly. Pulling with it only made it slightly easier. It went on forever. Eventually my arms ached and my gloved fingers burned. I had to rest.

I reached for the rest of the yam with arms that quaked from fatigue. The nerves jumped like fish springing up from a pond. *You simply need nourishment.* I ate the yam and a couple of dates, washing them down with some sips from the flask. I'd rest a moment, my head against the wall…just to gather strength. But nail-pulling was more tiring that I'd considered. I closed my eyes and evened my breath. Then darkness.

I awoke to the wretched blackness I'd encountered the morning before. *Damn!* The candle had burned out. The pinkish light from the door told me it was morning. That and the trill of winter birds. I'd slept through what remained of the night. I heaved up from the floor and felt my way over.

Running my fingers over the hinges, I located the one where I'd left the heart pendant hooked. My weak attempts in darkness were futile. *Did I really defile my mother's resting place for nothing?* A tear escaped.

Tracing back to my corner, I spent the long cold day wondering about Ichabod and Violet and if the Horseman would return tonight.

* * *

The rim of light had long faded when I him heard him at the door. I buried any fear, determined to get answers. He tromped in holding another bag along with a woolen blanket. He flung them toward me, then sweeping over to Father's coffin, he instantly lit one, two, three, four candles. My eyes squinted against the sudden light.

I rose, working to keep my breath steady. "How long are you planning to keep me here?"

He remained by the candles, dallying, passing his finger in and out of a flame. That only served to annoy me more. I stomped my foot. "You can't do this! I'll die in here."

With the swiftness of a fox, he charged around the coffins. I didn't know if he meant to attack me or storm out. But he came to an abrupt halt when his boot met with one of the nails left lying on the floor. He knelt, retrieved the bent thing, then turned to the hinges where the heart still hung. With an unsteady hand, he lifted it from its hook.

Damn!

With a rage that shook the whole room, he charged, whipping out his sword and fixing the tip to my neck. The heat of his anger descended the blade, biting into my flesh.

I did not yowl or cry or even waver. Instead, I stared into the nothingness that should've been his face. With clenched teeth, I hissed, "I sent you away."

He pressed the tip a little tighter, his hand trembling in a battle for control. I remained rock hard, chin up, daring him to employ the blade. Once his trembling grew to a quake, he whirled away. Sheathing his sword, he started for door.

"Wait! No! You can't leave me like this." Though obviously he could. His hand was already on the handle. I snatched up two of the crabapples and hurled one, then another, bouncing off his back. "Why are you doing this to me? Tell me!"

He spun back around. *Because you were seen!*

I flopped back against the wall, my mouth agape. Like a whisper in my ear, he'd spoken. Just like the times he'd called out my name. "Wh-What do you mean?"

Instead of answering he opened the door, the heart clutched in his fist.

"Stop! You can't leave now. And you certainly can't take my mother's pendant!"

But he was already gone.

I waited in the silence, wondering if he'd have a change of heart. *He has no heart.*

I staggered over to Father's coffin and blew out two of the candles, reminding myself that this time I'd have the good sense to light one from another before falling asleep. If I could sleep.

The Horseman's words echoed through me. *You were seen.*

By whom?

Wrapping myself into the much cherished blanket, I squatted back in my little crook in the corner. I glanced at the newest bag of provisions. At least I wouldn't starve here.

But I will most assuredly go mad.

* * *

The thin light from the door served as my timekeeper. That, and melting candles. I spent every agonizing minute watching the light grow and fade. The candles dwindled down. But I knew when night fell, he'd return.

I wiled away the time conjuring ways to overpower him, disarm him of his sword and run him through. Merely dreams, of course. Musings intended to satisfy my anger and give me a small taste of self-satisfaction. I wasn't blind to the fact I had no power whatsoever over this sword-wielding ghost.

The second candle had shrunk, its wax spread when I next heard him. He entered solemnly this night. He lit more candles, threw a small bag toward me, and dropped down to the floor, his back against the door. He sat, elbow propped on knee, like a close friend who'd just dropped in for a chat. Still, his presence overpowered me.

I didn't attempt to plead or shout or show any emotion, other than dejection, which I'd imagine he expected. Seconds passed into minutes. I kept my eyes lowered, staring down like a neglected doll.

Finally, he spoke. *You were seen.*

I lifted my eyes toward him. "I don't understand."

At the grave...where you were digging. You were seen.

His voice was not that of a blood-thirsty tyrant, but rather a calm and elegant man. Or maybe there was a mechanism in my mind that worked like a sieve, refining it to my own taste.

"Seen by whom?"

By someone who'd kill you before you'd time to blink.

"I have many enemies here, Horseman."

Indeed.

"So rather than attack this person who meant to harm me, you chose to swoop me up and knocked me unconscious?"

He straightened his knee and crossed his ankles. *Yes.*

I tightened the blanket around me. "You can't keep me locked up here forever, you know."

It seems I can.

Was holding me prisoner not enough for him, he had to torture me with word games as well? "What do you want from me?"

He stayed rooted in place. No attempt to answer.

I rose to my knees, hoping not to look like a beggar. Though in my present state of dress and cleanliness, that would be exceptionally hard. Still, I had to reason with him. "Listen." I worked to keep my voice steady. "There are people who care about me—"

And people who don't.

"I only care about those who do."

Then remain here until it's safe to leave.

"And just how long will that be?"

He brushed some imaginary lint from his trousers. *Until the Council is satisfied that you are no longer in the vicinity.*

I dropped back on to my heels. The Council knew I was here? "Tell me, Horseman. Who saw me?"

You know already.

He could only mean one person. "The Magistrate?" How stupid I'd been to peek through the parlor window at him.

The Horseman heaved himself from the floor.

"Wait! You're not leaving, are you? I'm going mad here all alone."

Instead of walking out, he went to Mother's coffin and slid back the lid.

Oh, dear God! "What are you doing?"

He took Mother's heart pendant from a pocket and laid it gently inside. *Katrina, you're much too young and beautiful to be pilfering from the dead. That's four times now.*

"Three," I corrected. His bones, the diamonds, and Mother's coffin.

Strange...I remember you stealing a dead man's sword.

True. The sword that he carried was the one I'd stolen from the Magistrate's stores. Though I'd tossed it deep into the waters of the Hudson. What means he'd used to retrieve it, I would never know.

"You're right," I said. "I pilfered your grave and look where it's gotten me."

He ignored my remark, pushing the coffin lid back in place.

"I sent your bones scattering to the sea, and, yet, here you are. How is that? I sent you away."

We have stronger ties to a vicinity than just our earthly remains. He turned away and walked backed to the door. Gripping the handle, he said, *You have food and candles. I'll return when—*

"No!" I leapt forward, rushing and clutching his cape. "I cannot spend another moment here! Please!"

He reached down and wrested my hands from the cloth. *Would you rather spend an eternity in hell?*

"I demand you let me out!"

Yes...so demanding, aren't you, Katrina? Just like your father.

My blood simmered and my teeth clenched. "What do you know of my father?"

He flung open the door. *That he always got what he wanted.* With those words, he was gone again.

* * *

I couldn't bear the thought of opening Mother's coffin again, removing the pendant in hopes of escape. No more futile attempts to free myself. The Horseman didn't mean to kill me, but how long did he mean to keep me here? I tended the candles. Paced the room. When my stomach finally growled for food, I dumped the contents of the bag. The usual fruit, vegetables, dried meat and—*Oh my goodness!*—a small book plopped out. A book! I moved closer to the light to read the title. Shakespeare's sonnets. *Hallelujah!* I hugged it to my chest, tears falling. The binding was battered and pages loose, unlike the leather-bound copy in my Father's library. But at that moment, it was more treasured than the food. At last a means to escape my own thoughts.

Taking an apple, I sat under the candlelight of Father's coffin. And for the next hour, I read.

* * *

The rim of light from the door waxed and waned. I sat waiting on Father's coffin, book in hand.

He paused while stepping in, like he'd expected me to be cowering in my usual corner. Then, quietly, he closed the door and leaned against it.

I licked my finger, paged to Sonnet 66, and read:

Tired with all these, for restful death I cry,

As to behold desert a beggar born,

And needy nothing trimmed in jollity,

And purest faith unhappily forsworn,

And gilded honor shamefully misplaced,

And maiden virtue rudely strumpeted,

And right perfection wrongfully disgraced,

And strength by limping sway disabled,

And art made tongue-tied by authority,

And folly, doctor-like, controlling skill,

And simple truth miscalled simplicity,

And captive good attending captain ill.

Tired with all these, from these would I be gone,

Save that to die, I leave my love alone.

He'd remained leaning against the door, arms crossed and cocky. *Katrina, you are not going to die. Not in here anyway.*

"You don't know that."

You have provisions, a warm blanket, and a book to pass the time.

How could I make him understand? "I don't want any of that. I want to go home."

Tell me, then. Where exactly is home?

Easy enough. "With Ichabod. I belong with him. Please, let me return."

He was here, by the way. In Sleepy Hollow.

I wavered, blood draining from my face. Slowly, I rose. "What? He was here?"

With not the slightest hint of emotion he answered, *Just briefly. He wore a wide brimmed hat, low, to cover his face. He snooped around, then went, careful to avoid the townspeople.*

The flatness of his tone rankled me. I wanted to lunge and strangle him. If only he'd had a neck. "And you couldn't have knocked him unconscious too? Brought him here to be with me?"

His safety is not my obligation.

"And neither is mine! I never appointed you my guardian angel."

That's very true, Katrina. I'm no angel.

"Then please, explain. Why do you feel this need to protect me?"

Because there is much in my past that connects us.

I doubted every word of that. "How could I possibly be connected to you? In life, you were just a simple Hessian who lost his head."

In more ways than one.

His cavalier air bristled the hairs on my arms. "I whispered stories about you as a child. The slightest mention of you sent shivers through every child in Sleepy Hollow. Adults too."

A headless rider would've frightened me as a child as well.

"But you fought alongside the enemy. Murdered for profit. All for nothing. Look what price you've paid."

He stood tall, as though ready to strike. *You, stupid girl, have no idea what price I paid. What I endured.*

"Then enlighten me." I plopped back down on Father's coffin and crossed my knees. "I have nowhere to go."

Perhaps I do. He turned.

He'd get no pleading from me this time. "Go on then, my guardian angel. I'll remain here like a good little girl, in the company of my dead parents. I'll converse with them. Read to them. Father was never one for Shakespeare, but Mother loved Sonnet 18. It was her favorite." I flipped to the page. "Shall I compare thee to a summer's day? Thou art more lovely and—"

He roared, slamming his fist to the wall, nearly crumbling the stone. *Number 116!*

"What?" I asked, book clutched to my chest.

He slowly drew his hand away. *Her favorite sonnet was 116.*

* * *

I struggled to hold onto the book that now trembled in my shaky hands. "You knew my mother?"

He moved first one way then another, as though confused on which way to turn. Finally, he reached for the door. *I must go.*

"No." I shot over quickly and threw myself in front of it. "You will not leave until you tell me how you knew my mother."

He withdrew his sword and laid the blade to my neck. *I will come and go as I please.*

"Yes, a privilege I'm not afforded."

He held the sword firmly in place, his body quivering as much as mine.

What was it about me that riled him so?

"Is this it then, guardian angel? You're going to slice off my head? You only just told me I wouldn't die here."

He held the blade there a moment longer. Long enough for me to wonder if he'd had a change of heart. Then he pulled the sword away and backed off. I, however, remained between him and the door.

"Tell me how you knew my mother."

He sheathed the sword and sauntered over to her coffin. *I was an apprentice cooper to her uncle.*

An apprentice cooper? "Wait…you didn't come here to fight in the war?"

No, I came much earlier, to escape my contemptible family.

Were they as savage as he? "And you worked for my great-uncle?"

Yes. Anna had just come to live with his family the year before.

True. My mother came to stay with her uncle after her parents and two younger brothers were taken in a flood. I grew up hearing their stories. She'd never stopped mourning their loss.

"But you knew her favorite sonnet. You must've known her well."

He hesitated a moment. *I knew her better than anyone.* Sweeping back his cape, he whipped around. *Even better than you, though you may find that hard to comprehend.*

"Horseman, please…I am in no mood to parry insults."

And I am in no mood to rehash old times. Move away from the door so that I may depart.

"Not a chance."

I waited, assuming he'd shove me aside. But he remained where he was.

"So is that why I'm here? You feel a need to protect me over some long ago obligation to my mother?"

I wouldn't expect you to understand.

"Why? Do you think I've no obligations of my own? Right now there are four people whose happiness lies with me. I must help them."

By going to the gallows?

"I wouldn't have to. If you're so eager to help, carry me back to Philadelphia yourself."

So that you can continue hiding behind an alias? Not keep the name that Anna gave you?

"Why are you so set on this? What was my mother to you anyway?"

Everything.

Though he'd uttered it no louder than a whisper, the word resounded through the tomb with an affection that could warm the coldest hearts. "You loved her?"

Like no other.

"But she didn't love you." She couldn't have. Mother had always looked upon Father with a softness and smile in her eyes. He'd been the love of her life.

She loved me, he said, sorrow in this words. *As much as I loved her. And we held on to that love, even up to the end.*

The end? "The end of what?"

He twisted away, his hands clenching. *Stop it, Katrina. Speaking of her while she's in the room reeks of sacrilege.*

"It's only her bones, you fool. Don't you think if she were truly in the room, she'd have already opened this door and let me out? What reeks is the position you've placed me in." I slid down the door and plopped myself firmly on the floor. Then rolling my hand, I gestured, "Continue. Tell me of

141

your devotion to Mother." It's not like I had anywhere to go. And, yes, I admit, I was intrigued.

What do you care?

"I care greatly. She was my mother."

We were two people in love. But Alwin...your uncle, was never one for sentiment. He was a sharp business man, and she was leverage.

"Leverage?"

Your father had already built his fortune. He sought a wife to bear an heir. Anna had accompanied Alwin on many of his trips to the Van Tassel farm, so it was no surprise that Baltus fell in love with her too.

"But if she loved you..."

Alwin struck a deal with Baltus. Anna was the bargaining chip.

No. That couldn't be. Mother loved Father. Only Father. Still... "Why did you not fight for her?"

Oh, I fought. Tooth and nail. She fought too. Did you ever meet Alwin?

"I only saw him once, when I was small."

Then you would've seen the patch over his eye. The Horseman began to pace, brushing his hand along Mother's coffin. *Anna did that. I should've killed him right then.*

I tried to visual it. That soft sweet woman and her gentle smile, growing rabid, clawing into her uncle—a rage fueled by love. In all my years she'd barely even raised her voice. "You couldn't run away together?"

After the brawl I was badly injured—a deep cut to my ribs. As I lay recovering, several men broke in. They bound and gagged me and carted me to a forest miles north of here. There, they left me tied me to a tree. Nearly two full days I was restrained, the coarse burlap gag drying to my tongue. I was barely conscious when some woodcutters happened by. It took four days after that to gain enough strength to journey back. By then, Anna was gone. There was also a warrant for my arrest, Alwin accusing me of gouging his eye.

I fought back any feelings of compassion. In life, this man had been a butcher. A savage. I'd not pity him or his prior situation. "But you must've seen her again...known about me."

Only later. After losing her, I wandered down to New York City for a time.

A sad story, but water under the bridge. "So please, enlighten me. At what point did my mother ask you to keep watch over *me?* To be my sworn protector?"

Again, his fist clenched. *Don't you understand? You are her child. The only part of her left. She'd want you to remain safe.*

"Then where were you while I was jailed last year? They meant to hang me, you know."

"There were others seeing to your escape then. There is only me to help you now."

I threw up my hands. "So you think leaving me imprisoned in this freezing tomb with only cold food, water,

143

and a book—one I have fully memorized—is helping me? I honestly can't believe what I'm hearing." Removing those nails had been easier than reasoning with this ghost.

You're hearing nothing, you foolish girl. You have a head yet refuse to use it.

"I don't know what you want from me!"

He thundered toward me, the heat of his ire preceding him. *A little gratitude, perhaps?*

I recoiled as he lashed out, kicking me aside. He stormed out, slamming the door so hard the rush of air flickered the candles.

I picked myself up, straightening my clothes. "Is he right, Mother?" I said to her coffin. "Is this what you want?"

Nothing but empty silence.

* * *

I dragged myself back to my corner, my mind astir. *Ichabod.* The Horseman's words echoed in my head. *Just briefly. He wore a wide brimmed hat, low, to cover his face. He snooped around, then went, careful to avoid the townspeople.* I buried my face in my palms. "Oh, Ichabod. I broke my promise. I'm so sorry."

Tears welled. If I don't get out, he may never know what became of me. Was his heart slivered into a thousand pieces? Like mine. *Like Anna's? Like the Horseman's?*

Sleep came and went in restless spurts. I paced. I read. But mostly, I thought. Standing between my parents' coffins,

I glanced from one to the other. Father had loved her. I know he had. But he was never one to show emotion. And Mother? If she didn't love him at first, she'd learned to. But theirs had been a marriage of convenience—forced upon her by a greedy uncle.

She'd loved the Horseman.

And we held on to that love, even up to the end.

He said he'd seen her later, after I was born. But when? And where? I yearned to know more. A thousand questions formulated in my head. And I held onto each till nightfall…when the Horseman returned.

* * *

He blustered in that evening empty-handed, leaving the door opened wide. *You're free to go.*

My mouth gaped as I blinked surprise. I cautiously rose. "What?"

The Magistrate has relaxed the search. The night guards are no longer patrolling. If you leave by the back roads, you won't be seen.

His words were neither hurried nor casual. Just pure statement of, what I hoped to be, fact.

All those questions I'd amassed fizzled away. Free? I was free! "But what about my horse?"

Watered, rested, and waiting under the bridge.

"Oh, thank you!" I touched my hand to my bodice, feeling the diamond-filled handkerchief tucked within. Then wrangling up the remaining food and water, I stepped out into the sweet night air. Ah... Pure medicine for my suffering lungs. I inhaled as though it were in limited supply.

The Horseman handed me the book of sonnets. *Have a long and fruitful life, Jane Hanover.* He turned and went back into the tomb.

Yes, I should've been in a race to the bridge, but I paused instead. Jane Hanover. Though there'd been no clear indication in his tone, I felt the use of that name was meant to manipulate me—to reach me on some emotional level. A reminder that, yes, I'd continue hiding behind an alias, not keeping the name Anna had given me. But no matter what I'm called, there were people right now who needed me, depended on me, ached for me. Still... I peeked back through the door. The Horseman stood by Mother's coffin, his hand resting on the lid. "What are you not telling me?"

He kept his back to me. *What do you mean?*

"You refused to take me back to Philadelphia because I'd live out my life as Jane. But I have no other choice. I either live a lie or hang."

Or clear your name.

Still more word games. "And how do you suppose I do that?"

He tapped a finger to the coffin lid, then turned. *By asking the right questions.*

As badly as I wanted to go, I knew there was more reason to stay. I stepped back into that foul-smelling hole and gently closed the door. "What are the right questions?"

He gave a slight shrug, an awkward gesture for someone missing a head. *You're not the least bit curious why the man who accused you of witchcraft and placed you under arrest confiscated your farm?*

My farm. Or it would've been upon Father's death. "Magistrate Harding is the most powerful man in the village. I'm sure he persuaded the notary to draw up some sort of legal papers."

Harding, he said, as though an afterthought.

Too curious, I set my things aside. "What do you know? Are you suggesting I could get my farm back?"

He waggled a finger at me. *Now you're asking the right questions.*

"And what would you propose? That I shoot the magistrate?"

He chuckled. *A tempting solution.*

"Do you have another?"

He stepped closer to me, a move I interpreted as a "pay attention" gesture.

The acreage Harding owned here in Sleepy Hollow was signed over to him while he still resided overseas. That was about twenty years ago.

"You knew him personally?"

Harding? No. I only encountered him once, during my time in the *city. The night he was murdered.*

"Murdered? That makes no sense. Harding lives here."

Does he?

"Yes. I assure you that man is no ghost."

True. But is he Harding?

I stopped, considering his implication. "What are you saying?"

Harding was murdered and robbed—all his money and papers *stolen. The man you know—the one who presides over the Hollow—is* *nothing but a cutthroat and a bandit. A worthless imposter.*

"And you know this as fact? You were there?" A vein in my neck twitched as my heart beat sped. Though I'd not let hope consume me as yet.

The Horseman leaned a shoulder to the wall. *His real* *name is Orrick Mendel, a German immigrant. He arrived in New* *York a few weeks before Harding. Orrick and I shared lodging during* *that time.*

"So you fell into bad company."

Not so much fell *into it. It followed me.*

"Followed you?"

Yes. An aura of contempt surrounded him. *Orrick is my* *brother.*

His words hit hard and I locked my knees for support. He'd told me yesterday that he'd come from Germany to
148

escape his contemptible family. "You knew what he was like. Why would you want to share a room with him?"

Keep in mind, Katrina, this was not long after I'd lost Anna. My despondency had hardened to bitterness. Fate had cheated me like a sharper. I no longer cared.

"No longer cared? You abetted a criminal. Being lovelorn is one thing, but aiding a loathsome—"

He stomped even closer, now mere inches away, and placed his hand to the hilt of his sword, partially exposing the blade. *Would you stop being your father's daughter for at least five seconds so I may help you?*

Though I knew it to be an empty threat, I stepped several paces back, my hands raised.

He closed the sword back into place and huffed a sigh. *I was lonely. Orrick was company. We spent our evenings at the tavern, drinking and gambling*—he paused as though recalling—*fondling the wenches.*

"Pardon the interruption," I dared, "but there are some details best kept to yourself."

It happened in August, he continued, like the story benefited him more than me. *We stumbled out late and down to the harbor. The passenger ship Minerva had just moored and its passengers disembarked. Orrick and I had gambled away all our money, so we meant to take a wallet or two. Then we saw Harding…alone, carrying bags in each hand. The idiot came right up to us, asking where he might*

149

find lodging for the evening. Orrick gave him directions to a nearby inn. Keeping to the shadows, we followed.

The Horseman resumed his position against the wall. If he had eyes they'd likely have been downcast. *We only meant to rob him at gunpoint, take his money and go. But the fellow was quicker than we thought. He rushed us, the gun fired, and Harding's brains met the brick wall behind him.*

Another detail I could've done without.

Frightened, we took his things and ran. We didn't slow until we were back in our room. That's where we discovered Harding was an extremely wealthy man. Not just money. Inside his bags we found an expensive pocket watch, a small purse with silver, and the deed to the property in Sleepy Hollow.

Orrick saw it as a lucky turn. A chance to make more of himself. He'd take Harding's place. Live his life and abandon the dregs of his past.

"And he didn't offer to split it with you?"

I was looked upon as one of those dregs. He did give me some of the money. But he couldn't take me with him, insisting we end ties.

"Why couldn't he?"

Because Anna was here. That risked exposure. He said if I followed, he'd report the murder. Have me arrested.

"Have you arrested? That's ridiculous. You were both in on it."

The Horseman hesitated, scraping his boot heel to the wall. *I'm the one who held the pistol.*

"But you came here. Died here."

Yes. A few years later I happened upon a camp of Hessian soldiers and took up their cause. The war brought me back to Sleepy Hollow. By then I was bitter and broken—killing was a release. With every soldier I slayed I saw Alwin or Orrick—he gestured toward Father's coffin—*even Baltus.*

"That's when you saw Mother again. And me."

You looked so much like her, standing near the village square, holding her hand. I kept a distance, but I could see her clearly. She was more beautiful than ever. And she still wore the pendant I'd given her.

"Wait…You gave her? I thought it had belonged to her mother?"

No. It had belonged to my *mother. My heart broke all over again. Anyway, the next day I went into battle. That day was my last.*

I wondered how many Continental soldiers were slaughtered that day because of his broken heart. "But even in death you continued to murder."

Only when necessary.

"Necessary? You killed Old Brower and Cornelius Putnam. What had they ever done to you?"

At that moment he appeared more weary than I—as though he'd been the one locked away with only a little food, water, and a corner to relieve himself.

They did nothing to me, Katrina. They had a beef with Baltus, claiming he'd cheated them somehow. Most likely true. The last statement uttered under his breath. *They conspired a plot to make him pay. And in their eyes, only one thing was more valuable than his money.*

I waited for more. When it didn't come I asked, "Me? Is that why you came to me back then? To warn me?"

Yes.

"Is that also why you came to me in Philadelphia? To tell me of Harding?"

Yes.

I threw my hands up, heat filling my face. "Then why did you not just tell me? You drew your sword. You poked my neck!" I jutted my chin and placed my fingers to the fading nick.

It's hard to reason with a maniac swinging a fire poker.

"I was frightened."

Exactly. You wouldn't have trusted the ghost that fueled your nightmares as a child.

Not only as a child.

Had I spoken then, you wouldn't have listened.

"No. You're right. But as much as I hate Harding, and want what is legally mine, I have no proof that he's someone else. Who would even listen to such a story?"

Orrick's a terribly vain man. I can assure you, Katrina, he's kept his immigration papers and passport as an amusing reminder that he's hornswoggled an entire village. I know my brother. His arrogance exceeds common sense. If you can somehow get inside his house, you'll find the papers will be locked away there.

He made it sound so simple. But wait... Maybe it was! "You could do that for me. You come and go here all the time."

He waved it off. *He's had the house warded against the supernatural. I cannot enter.*

So much for simple. "You seem quite confident that I can accomplish this."

You can.

"But think about it. What if I am caught?" I arched a brow. "You will have put Anna's child in danger."

He retrieved my bag and held it toward me. *Then I suggest you don't get caught.*

* * *

Without another word, the Horseman breezed past, leaving me all alone.

I replayed those final words. *Then I suggest you don't get caught.* I wouldn't. I couldn't. That would be like a slap to his face...if he had one. I took another glance at my parents' coffins. I owed it to them as well. "I won't get caught." *There's room here for another coffin if I do.* No! I pushed the thought aside, gathered myself, and stole out into the silent night.

As the Horseman promised, Dewdrop waited under the bridge. How wonderful to see her again. The leather satchel still hung from the saddle. I quickly pulled the diamonds from my bodice and tucked them inside it. Then mounting, I said, "Let's go, girl." With a snap of the reins, we rode away—away from the cemetery to the one place I trusted. The one place I knew I'd get a good night's sleep.

* * *

Around noon the next day, I sneaked inside my Van Tassel mansion. Yes, I kept to the thinking that it was still my home. The knife lay concealed under my cloak even though I knew the magistrate would be off in town, throwing his authority around and making someone who'd committed lesser crimes than his own pay dearly. *What price will you pay, Harding?*

Managing to elude two servants, I skulked into what was once my father's office, barely recognizable now. Father's mahogany desk had been replaced with an elaborately carved pedestal version, complete with a studded-leather wingback chair. I doubted even President Washington signed papers on anything this majestic. Of course if the villagers had ransacked the house while I was jailed, they would've taken everything of value, including the furniture. But no time for sentimentalities. I began my search, combing through every drawer of that elephantine desk.

The fact that not a single one was locked should've alerted me that the evidence wouldn't be there, though I found a few things among his filings that I thought should stay under lock and key. These included folios of an erotic nature, sketches of saturnalia, and a crude printing of a novel entitled *Memoirs of a Woman of Pleasure* by John Cleland. *Ick. I want to know nothing of your carnal interests!*

Since the desk failed to provide the papers, I swept over to a corner secretaire. I pulled at the tambour door. Latched. *Aha.* I scurried back to the desk and retrieved a pearl-handled letter opener. *How I wished I had this when I was first locked in the tomb!* Without regard for the value of the secretaire—and it did look expensive—I pried and twisted until I'd broken the lock free. The tambour easily rolled up, revealing a great lot of nothing. A chipped figurine, a dried inkwell, sealing wax, and a pair of spectacles minus a lens. The only paper items were a few maps and plats that looked to be a useless bunch of junk. I reached up to close the tambour. *God, please let those papers be in this office.* The thought of searching his bedroom was too much to bear.

Just before pulling it down, my eyes fell to something a bit off. Fingerprints. Several pudgy ones on the upper back panel. Why on earth would anyone need to touch the back

155

inside wall of this secretaire? I tapped it. Hollow. My heart kicked at the possibility.

Placing my fingers over the prints, I pushed. The panel stayed firmly in place. I stupidly tried sliding it, even though I could clearly see there was no place for it to shift. Then I pushed down. The top portion popped loose from its groove and fell like cut timber against my hand. I caught it before it could do further damage to the already broken items he kept here. Decoys, I realized. But on the other side of that panel— *I knew it!*—two things were revealed to me. A small document box, locked, and a large lump of something bundled in linen. I snatched up the box and shook it. *Aha!* The shifting of papers rattled inside. I'd have to break into it somehow, but at least now I had access to tools. Regardless, I was *more* than certain this was my proof.

Of course there was that other hidden thing to consider. The lump. It had to be important. Why else would it be here? *What other secrets have you concealed, you scoundrel?* I leaned near it and untied the top. The four corners of cloth fell open and the empty sockets of a human skull met my gaze. *Oh no!* My breathing grew rough as my chest rose and fell. *Orrick, how could you?* I took the skull in my hands for examination. "You killed your own brother?" That's when I heard the click. I turned to find a pistol leveled between my eyes.

"Yes," the magistrate said from the other end of the barrel, "I killed my own brother. No loss of course. He'd always been a stubborn fool."

Now I couldn't help but wonder, had the Horseman sent me because I was Anna's daughter or because he sought revenge? Though, honestly, I don't think he knew at whose hands he fell.

The magistrate gnawed at his lip, considering me. "You've left me with a hefty decision, Katrina. Kill you on the spot or bask in the laurels of your capture."

Still holding the Horseman's skull, I considered smashing it over the magistrate's. Too chancy. I'd likely find a bullet through my own. "I'm sure the townspeople are hungry for me. Why deny yourself the glory of delivering me to them?"

"They're more than hungry, my dear, they're ravished. The townsfolk will rip you to shreds. Especially now that you have Brom's blood on your hands."

"I did not kill Brom."

"I don't care."

"Well, you wouldn't, now would you, *Orrick*?"

He ground his teeth. "As I feared, you've been consorting with ghosts."

"He wouldn't be a ghost if you hadn't murdered him."

"I'd warned him to stay away. My life was set. I was Harding. I wouldn't have him spoil my good fortune."

Chancing it, I said, "Yes, wait till I tell the townspeople about that."

"No one will listen to your ravings, Katrina." He nodded toward the document box. "Especially since all evidence will soon be destroyed. It would simply be your word against mine."

That's when another pistol appeared, the barrel pressed to the back of the magistrate's head. "No, Harding," Notary de Graff said, "it would be *our* word against yours." The pistol cocked. "Katrina, take his gun."

I ducked away, set the Horseman's head down and disarmed the swindler.

Orrick held his hands over his head. "You're making a mistake, de Graff."

The notary held firm. "No mistake. Katrina told me the whole story last night. I now know who really murdered my son...and why. And I know all about you. I'm grateful she came to me."

And I was grateful to him. He'd trusted me. Believed me. And because of him, I was able to take a much cherished bath and sleep on a soft bed—though his dead wife's dress did bag around me.

"Grab the box," the notary said to me. "I'll keep it under safekeeping"—he poked the gun harder at Orrick, causing the charlatan to squint—"until his trial."

Orrick snarled at me. "I should've opened that cell door and let the people devour you."

A smile curled the corners of my mouth. "Which proves once again, Magistrate, you make very poor choices."

Part Three

July 1794

I contemplated the many boxes and bags waiting on the floor of the master bedroom and raised an eyebrow to Ichabod. He appeared a bit harried with his vest unbuttoned, his white shirtsleeves rolled at the cuffs. "Do you think I over packed?" I asked.

He wore a *how are we going to fit it all?* look as well. With a smile, he drew me into his arms and laid a kiss on my forehead. "I'm just happy we're transporting it in advance. Otherwise we'd be perched on those hatboxes the entire trip."

I was immediately struck with an image of Ichabod "perched," his knees to his chest. That brought a smile to my own lips. "Sooo...too many hats?"

He gave me a gentle squeeze. "You can never have too many hats."

True.

"But don't worry," he continued, "I'm sure the men can manage to fit it all into the dray."

The men Ichabod referred to were paid servants, many of which were former Van Tassel slaves. Emancipating them had been my first priority once the farm reverted back to me.

He ran his fingers along my spine, sending waves of tingles throughout me. "Just one more day," he said. Then brushing back my hair, he kissed me—something he'd done multiple times daily since our wedding. Far too many times for me to count. But why bother? I'd never tire of him or his delicious kisses.

Yes, one more day. That's when we'd leave Sleepy Hollow and move back to Philadelphia. Ichabod had secured an excellent position to study law with a more prestigious firm. And rather than sell the farm, we found an excellent overseer to manage in our absence. Money would be no problem. No, we wouldn't be living on Society Hill, but we wouldn't be languishing in squalor either.

We were immersed in a passionate kiss when a slight knock sounded at our open bedroom door. "Ahem."

Only our lips parted, not our eyes. *Oh, how I love those eyes.* "Yes, Violet," I said.

"If you and Zachary could pry yerselves away from each other for five seconds—"

Ichabod rolled his eyes and tilted his head toward her. "Are you ever going to call me Ichabod?"

Her lip twitched. "Not likely. Anyway, I need to know what Katrina wants to do about the doll."

My name never seemed a problem for her since it was so very much like her own. She admitted to never liking her real name – Katereena. It's just as well. Using Violet avoided confusion.

"Oh, the doll," I said. She meant Jonas's automaton, now completed and performing beautifully. His wedding gift to us.

I admit, I'd left him brokenhearted, but fully and completely without debt. At first he'd been too proud to accept the money, but I convinced him it was money owed to him—money to make up for my deception, Seth's arm, and for the kindness he and his mother had shown me.

Oh, and I did get a formal written apology from Seth, saying how sorry he was for the *misunderstanding*. I didn't reply. Nor did I go near him again after setting the story straight. The wretch actually tried to convince Jonas that I'd purposely pushed him over the stairs when he wouldn't carry through on my sexual advances. *"I couldn't betray you, dear brother."* The worm! Though beautifully written, I didn't feel his apology was heartfelt. Especially since it came with an added thank you for breaking his arm. Who knew that one-handed juggling would sell even more pies?

"Never mind about the doll, Violet. It's going to ride in the coach with me tomorrow. I couldn't live with myself if it were to break."

"Ah, don't worry," she said. "If it does ya have Jonas close by to fix it."

As she turned to go, I stepped out of Ichabod's embrace. "Are you sure you won't change your mind and come with us?"

Her lip curled like I'd suggested she eat raw possum. "Nay. My job is here, lookin' after yer house. And I do love this farm so much."

I glanced from her to Ichabod and back. "Is it really the farm you love or young Abram?" Abram Smit. One of the local boys. A year older than Violet. He constantly found excuses to visit our farm these days.

She blushed the color of her hair. "It ain't about that."

It was. Though when she wasn't managing the house, you could find her in the stables or the barn, petting the newborn lambs and yellow chicks. She was definitely a farm girl at heart.

"Invite him to dinner tonight," Ichabod said. "A small party before our departure."

Her grin nearly reached her ears. "All right. And we'll do it up fancy too."

I gave a stern nod. "Fancy, it is." Then hurrying to her, I reached out and hugged her close.

"I'm gonna miss ya so much," she whispered against my ear.

"I'll miss you too. But only for a few months. I'll be back at harvest to check up on things."

"Right," she said, looking down at me with soft eyes. Then, snapping back to her old self, she dropped her arms from around me. "I need to get word to Abram about dinner.

And plan the menu." Her voice faded as she walked off. "But no chickpeas. He hates chickpeas."

When I turned back, Ichabod was standing behind me. He carried a box in one hand and two bags in another. "The men will be arriving soon to load up. Might as well get a head start."

"Would you like some help?" I asked.

Balancing the baggage, he placed a light kiss on the tip of my nose. "I'm sure you have plenty of other pressing matters…last minute and all."

Yes…one in particular.

* * *

It was about three when I hitched Dewdrop to a low limb and removed a key from my pocket. The lock easily tumbled open. I swung the door wide and, for my own assurance, placed a rock at its base to hold it in place. The summer sun cast a warm glow into the tomb. How different it looked in daylight. Other than some moss sprouting in the corner and a cobweb spread on the angel's wings, the small room looked rather quaint.

After setting the valise I carried on the floor, I carefully pushed aside Mother's coffin lid. This time, I did not avert my eyes. Unbuckling the valise, I spread it open and removed the two items inside. First, the Horseman's skull. It had remained locked in the courthouse evidence room even after Orrick's trial and execution. With a little persuading to the jailer, it came into my possession yesterday. I laid the skull next to Mother's so that their heads would meet. In her hand I placed the tattered book of sonnets, open to 116.

"Mother, I cannot give you the life you should've had. This is the best I can do. But I love you and miss you. I always will."

I closed the lid, picked up the valise, and said a goodbye to Father too. Then, locking the door, I rode away content. No more lies. No more secrets. Well...except for five. The diamonds. Since the notary wasted no time signing Father's wealth back over to me, I had no reason to sell them. Still wrapped in the handkerchief, they're hidden away. And only I know where they are kept.

Other Books by Dax Varley

SPELLBOUND AND DETERMINED

Welcome to Mimi's Charms & Enchantments—a New Age shop filled with magical merchandise and colorful customers. Cam couldn't ask for a better afterschool job.

When a shady man in gray slinks in one afternoon, Cam is *thisclose* to calling 911. To her relief, he hurries away, leaving behind the nauseating odor of his cologne and a curious spell he's dropped on the floor. But this spell is not your average hocus-pocus. It's ancient, odd and promises *Power Supreme*—something Cam could definitely use to keep up her 3.9 grade point average.

But the spell requires more than what's stocked on Mimi's shelves. And acquiring each item will take some heavy teamwork. With the help of her best friend, Reade, and Zach, the high school's resident genius/nerd, Cam can't lose...unless the Gray man returns.

LOST GIRL (an Oracles novelette)

Juniper Lynch has a flair for all things psychic - a gift she inherited from her dearly departed granny.

When her best friend, Gena needs help finding her missing retainer, Juniper is quick to try scrying, aka crystal-gazing. With no crystal ball handy, she goes the easy route and gazes into a glass of water. But the image that appears is not what she expected. The shriveled face of a missing girl floats to the surface. Juniper is seized by a mystical connection and the countdown clock begins.

Can she find the lost girl before they both wither away?

SECOND SIGHT (an Oracles novelette)

Gena Richmond is a collector of shades...sunglasses, that is. Every size, shape, color and style. So when she finds an unusual pair at a secondhand shop, it's love at first sight. But these glasses are more than simple sun-blockers. They show her visions of what's to come...and what's coming is heart-stopping horrific.

Katrina is still haunted by her encounter with the Headless Horseman—the night he beckoned to her. Now he has risen again, slashing heads and terrorizing the quiet countryside.

Her only joy during this dismal darkness comes when Ichabod Crane, a gorgeous young man from Connecticut, moves to Sleepy Hollow and their attraction turns to romance.

When the Horseman marks Ichabod as his next victim, Katrina, despite dangerous efforts to save him, sees no other choice than for them to flee.

But the Horseman awaits.

Now it's up to her to sever the horror and alter the Legend of Sleepy Hollow.

Dax Varley writes the kind of young adult novels she wishes were around when she was a teen. She's a lover of humor, horror and all things paranormal.

When Dax isn't writing, she's collecting odd photos online, reading recaps of her favorite shows or kicked back with a good book. She lives in Richmond, Texas with her husband, a shelf full of action figures and about a dozen imaginary friends.

Real or imaginary, you can find her at the following locations:

DaxVarley.com

Twitter: @daxvarley

Facebook.com/DaxVarley

CPSIA information can be obtained at www.ICGtesting.com
Printed in the USA
LVOW10s0744081014

407820LV00001B/75/P